SPEAK NOW

SPEAK NOW

A Modern Novel

Frank Yerby

THE DIAL PRESS, INC.
NEW YORK 1969

Library of Congress Catalog Card Number: 74-91119
Printed in the United States of America
Book Design by Thomas Clemens
First Printing, 1969

For
Anna Bontemps

A NOTE TO THE READER

This is a novel about miscegenation—one of the two or three ugliest and most insulting words in the English language—for when a man and a woman of different races decide to join their lives, their fortunes, and their sacred honors, who (unless it be Hypothetical and *soi-disant* Almighty God) has the right or the arrogance to decide which of them misses, and which cegenates, as it were?

To those readers who find this theme uncongenial, this is where this novel ends.

To those readers who really don't believe in the novel, or in any writer's creativity, and try always to reduce the long and lonely suffering it takes to claw a work of art (whatever its quality!) up out of the guts of one's subconscious to biography, or what is even worse, autobiography, the writer can only say to them, have fun.

For the characters in this novel all lived, somewhere, some time. They all did approximately what the writer has made them do in these pages. He has known three Harrys and four Kathys well, even intimately, each of whom has contributed a word, a trick of speech, a mute gesture, a single cry of anguish to this work. But none of them *is* the Harry or the Kathy of this book. By which the writer means that he is a novelist and this is a novel.

Read it as such—or not at all.

F. Y.

"If there be any person present who knows of a valid reason why this man and this woman should not be joined in the bonds of Holy Wedlock, let him speak now, or forever henceforth hold his peace."

THE WEDDING CEREMONY

Chapter
One

"Now you," the policeman said. "Documents!"

Harry put his hand inside his jacket and came out with the billfold. It wasn't a billfold, really, although it looked like one. It was what the French call a *porte-documents*, a kind of leather pack with many clear plastic divisions into which you crammed all the permits you needed in order to live and work in Paris. Out of simple curiosity, Harry had once dumped them all onto the scale in the butcher shop of his quarter; and they had come to slightly less than two hundred and fifty grams, almost a quarter of a kilo. "Liberty, equality, and bureaucracy," the butcher had said.

The policeman looked at them one by one, jotting down their numbers: permit to conduct a coach of motor of explosions; permit to sojourn in the City of Paris; permit special extended by the Syndicate of Musicians, Department of the Seine, to work as a musician in a club of night, with the added note that the self-called club of night was property of a subject foreign, and the here-joined permit issued at the request of the owner; card of registration with the Embassy of the States United of America, which caused the agent of the Sûreté to look at Harry in another way. The prescribed Gaullist official manner; frosty as an Eskimo's conception of hell, Harry decided.

"You are an American, then?" he said.

"Yes, Mister the Agent," Harry said, speaking very slowly and clearly and employing deliberately the somewhat baroque usages of emphasis that Frenchmen use habitually. "But that is not my fault, is it? My ancestors did not invite themselves aboard the vessels of the Slavers, nor choose the country to which they were sent. Given a choice, they would have stayed in Africa. My connection, then, with the Anglo-Saxon bloc is, one could say, involuntary . . ."

Mister the Agent permitted himself an almost smile.

"Nor have you any connections with the countries of Africa of the North, I suppose?" he said.

"None," Harry said.

"And also, you know nothing of this affair of the shooting?"

"Solely what I saw," Harry said.

"And what is it that you saw?" the policeman said.

"A front-drive, type DS 19, gray," Harry said. "Three occupants: the driver and two other individuals, all of them of distinctly North African aspect, the two passengers armed with machine guns, small, the Sten type. The matriculation of the Citroën was 13 548 SM 75. Which will serve Mister the Agent for nothing, I am sure of that . . . "

"Why not?" the policeman said.

"Because the newness of the vehicle and the shabbiness of its occupants leads one inescapably to the conclusion the automobile was stolen," Harry said.

"There you are doubtless right," the plainclothes agent of the Sûreté said. "And you have a remarkable gift of observation as well. Continue please."

"When they stopped in front of the club," Harry said, "I was returning from having a sandwich and a glass of milk in the café across the street."

"Is it that you do not eat in the club?"

"No."

"We have not the discrimination racial in France," the policeman said. "So, if Monsieur Zahibuine has dared—"

"No," Harry said. "It is solely that the nourishment here at Le Blue Note is, she also, of the North African variety. My stomach declares a hunger strike immediately upon the mere sight of it. My stomach is very provincial, I'm afraid . . ."

"Your stomach is without doubt wise," the Sûreté man said. "Go on, please."

"They opened fire at a distance of seven meters, approximately," Harry said. "Evidently it was not their intention to kill anyone—except possibly Ahmad him-self. Mister the Agent will observe that all the bullets went through the upper parts of the windows, too high to hit people sitting down. Pierre, being a waiter, was, unhappily, standing up. Poor Pierre. He was a brave type. I shall miss him . . ."

"You hold the death of Monsieur Benoit an accident, then? He had never been—abusive toward North Africans, say?"

"Never," Harry said. "One does not mistreat people of the same nationality as one's patron, Mister the Agent. That would not be, it seems to me, wise . . ."

"Evidently. What then, Monsieur—" the agent con-sulted his notes—"Forbes, is your opinion of the motive of this affair?"

"If Mister the Agent will permit me to emphasize that it *is* opinion solely, I should say politics. Monsieur Zahibuine naturally does not confide in his employees. But upon several occasions I have seen him become angry and upset with visitors who entered his office. Very often, upon such occasions, there was shouting . . ."

"About what did they shout?" the agent said.

"Unhappily I do not speak or even comprehend Arabic," Harry said.

"I see. Continue with your account of the shooting," the plainclothesman said.

"They fired very carefully and coolly, destroying all the windows. Within there was much screaming and break-ing of tables and chairs as the guests threw themselves to the floor. But, as I said before, it was evidently not the intention of the freeshooters to kill anyone. The only person whom they seriously tried to eliminate was me, myself . . ."

"You?" the agent said.

"But yes. You see, at the last instant, they observed that I had seen them from a vantage point that might make it possible for me to identify them later—"

"And could you?" the policeman said.

Harry shrugged.

"It is as the whites of my country say of the people of my race—all North Africans look the same to me..."

"Go on," the agent said.

"So they expended two clips of twenty-five shots each with solely this result," Harry said, and held his clarinet case out to the policeman.

The agent looked at the case.

"Not bad. As shooting, well understood, I mean," he said. "How was it that you were not wounded?"

"Perhaps because the very amiable Army of Vietnam of the North, and their even more amiable friends, the Vietcong, provided me quite recently with incessant motives for ameliorating my agility corporal," Harry said. "In any event, the purchase of a new clarinet and case is more agreeable than having to buy a coffin would have been, is it not so, Mister the Agent?"

"True," the agent said. "You have nothing to add to your statement?"

"Nothing," Harry said.

"Very well. You understand that should you have occasion to leave Paris, or even to change your address within it, you are obliged to notify the Commissioner of Police . . . One thing more: It might be wise to ask the police of your district to provide you with a certain degree of surveillance . . . The members of El Fatah have been known to remove witnesses before now . . ."

"El Fatah?" Harry said.

"An organization of terrorists. Presently chiefly concerned with our Israeli friends . . ."

"But Ahmad—Monsieur Zahibuine—so far as I know—"

"Has absolutely no connection with the Israelis? Of course not. He merely became increasingly reluctant to contribute to El Fatah's fund dedicated to the purchase of arms."

The agent stopped. Frowned. Then he shrugged. The shrug was a work of art, a small, very Gallic masterpiece. It all but stated: "I have talked too goddamned much, but what's done is done, so now to repair the damage—"

"You understand, Monsieur Forbes," he said, "that I have given you this information merely to warn you that you might possibly be in some danger. You are not to divulge it to anyone . . ."

"D'accord," Harry said. "Thank you, Mister the Agent. May I go now?"

"Yes," Mister the Agent said. "And thank you infinitely for your cooperation, Monsieur Forbes . . ."

"Glad to have helped," Harry said. "That is, if I have . . ." Then he turned away from Le Blue Note, and walked toward the métro. He didn't walk any faster than usual, because when he walked too fast the calf of his right leg would begin to hurt him. It had been cut almost in half by a mortar shell fragment during a brisk firefight twenty miles north of A Shan, or about ten south of Hué, and although the limp it had left him with was almost unnoticeable, he'd learned from experience to favor that leg. For the same reason he usually played sitting down, even when it was his turn to solo. But he didn't think about his bad leg consciously anymore; he took the necessary precautions as a matter of habit, just as he'd learned to guard himself against self-torment on other levels as well: rootlessness, homesickness for a country even his willingly shed blood hadn't been able to buy him any meaningful part of, loneliness, his still new, raw, and absolutely appalling grief . . .

He put the Sûreté agent's warning in a niche in the back part of his brain and more than half forgot it. It wasn't that he was excessively brave; it was just that the advantages of life and consciousness over death and nothingness didn't seem that overwhelming anymore. He sat in his seat in the métro—at that hour of the morning there were always seats vacant on the subway cars—with his eyes closed until he came to his station. Then he got off, went up the long stairs, and came out into the gray fog that a pale, watery April sunlight was already trying to break through.

He sat down at a table in front of the same sidewalk café where he ate every morning and waited for the waiter to bring him the *café au lait complet* that he didn't even have to order anymore, because when Emil the waiter saw Harry sitting there, he'd bring it without being asked.

Harry sat there watching the traffic beginning to thicken along the boulevard, the cars outnumbering the trucks now, and the rumble of it rising. He was thinking that a mechanical civilization did unpleasant things to your insides and that any great city, even Paris, or maybe especially Paris, was unfit for human habitation; that is, if you granted the dubious proposition that there were any beings left who could truly be called human any-

more. Then he picked up his cup to drink his coffee
while it was still hot enough to be drinkable, and his
eyes met the girl's above the rim of the cup.

He didn't even hesitate.

"You're invited," he said, and turned toward the
doorway. "Emil, bring me another breakfast, if you
please—"

"*D'accord*, 'Arree," Emil said.

"No!" the girl said. "I—I couldn't accept—"

"Who asked you?" Harry said. "Now shut up and
eat. Starting with these croissants. Maybe they'll hold
you up 'til Emil gets back with your breakfast. You
pass out and I'll have to prove to the flics that it wasn't a
case of attempted rape, instead of a silly dame whose
allowance got held up and who hasn't eaten in three
days—"

"Four," the girl said, and started to cry.

"Cut that out," Harry said. "Come on over. No, don't.
I'll come over there."

He got up and moved over to her table, carrying his
breakfast with him.

"Now eat, damnit," he said.

He sat there watching her as she ate his breakfast,
then her own, and then another one he ordered for
her. He supposed that she was a very pretty girl; but all
his concepts of beauty had been changed by Fleur so
that this classic Nordic type seemed to him singularly
uninteresting, even dull. He saw his hand, so black that
it looked faintly bluish, lying on the table beside her
pale, freckled one, and smiled.

"Rent's paid up 'til when?" he said.

She stared at him, and he saw that she was afraid.
More than afraid: terrified. She had the kind of a drawl

that hadn't even a hint of a poorwhite's nasal whine in it, so he knew that she'd never, before this precise instant, exchanged two words with a Negro who hadn't a butler's or a chauffeur's uniform, or maybe a gardener's overalls on, in all her life.

"I asked you a question," he said.

Instead of answering, she bent her head and started crying again.

He looked down at her miniskirt, at her bare legs. Both needed washing.

"How many nights have you been sleeping in the métro?" he said.

"Two," she whispered.

"And la concierge kept your clothes, didn't she?"

"Yes. How'd you know all this, Mis—ter—?"

"Congratulations," Harry said.

"Congratulations? For what?" she said.

"For getting that 'Mister' out without choking to death on it. Not quite, anyhow. Now forget it. My name's Harrison Forbes. Call me Harry. All my friends do."

"All right. If you'll call me—Kathy. Katherine Nichols—"

"The tobacco people?"

"Yes. How'd you know?"

"I read the newspapers. Now tell me, how'd *you* happen to run out of money?"

He saw the color flare in her cheeks. Like that she *was* pretty. Very. And he saw another thing: She wasn't beaten yet. A simple thing like a breakfast—like three breakfasts, he corrected himself solemnly—and the fight was back.

"Ah, youth," he said.

She whirled on him then.

"Just what do you mean?" she said.

"I don't mean anything," he said slowly, "and I sometimes wonder if anybody ever does. Even when they think they do. Even when they're in there, trying. Now, forget it. None of my burrheaded, black, liverlipped business, Miss Anne! You're flat broke. You've been kicked out of your pad. You've been on a mighty strict diet. And you've been sleeping in the métro. That's enough. The why's don't matter a good goddamn—"

She sat there, looking at him; then, suddenly, impulsively, she put out her hand and let it rest on his arm.

"Now I *am* sorry," she said.

"Forget it," Harry said.

"No," she said. "I owe you an explanation. The truth is—I was robbed—"

"By someone you trusted," he said slowly.

"By someone I—loved," she said.

"Loved?" Harry said. "Past tense?"

Her head came up. That deadgame fighter's look was back in her eyes.

"Past tense," she said. "Definitely."

Harry studied her. He had the picture now, and it sickened him a little. He didn't know why the hell it should have, but it did. It happened every day in Paris to romantic little idiots out to live their lives. The girls who'd long since convinced the French—and the Italians, and the Spanish, and the Arabs, and all the other lesser breeds without the law, he thought wryly—that American women have the roundest heels in the universe . . . But there was one detail that didn't fit.

"Didn't he know who you are?"

"Of course," Kathy said.

"And he refrained from suggesting the old shoes, rice, and *Lohengrin* bit?"

"If you mean did he propose, yes. Constantly. I refused. Love isn't all *that* blind . . ."

"I see," Harry said.

"No, you don't. He was—my Paris boy. I just couldn't see myself bringing him home to Papa . . ."

"Or even picture him making the scene in Durham, North Carolina—"

"Exactly," Kathy said.

"So he took the cash, and let the credit go. Just as well. Good riddance to bad rubbish. But what doesn't figure in all this is why you didn't write, wire, or phone Pops for more lettuce—"

"Couldn't. I—I'd already had a letter from Papa telling me he wasn't going to be home for awhile. That he'd—that he'd gotten married—again. To a girl my age. They're honeymooning somewhere. Mexico, the Bahamas, God knows—and the only other people I could have written for money are the same ones who told Papa what a fool he was to let me come to France alone, anyhow, so—"

"I see," Harry said again.

"He has every right, I suppose," she whispered. "He's still quite young, he fought in the Second World War—"

"And you weren't born until after he got back," Harry said.

"I was supposed to represent—reconciliation," Kathy said. "Only it didn't work . . ."

Harry smiled at her then.

"I'd say it worked—just great," he said. "Now let's postpone the personal history 'til we've straightened you out. How much rent do you owe?"

"Two months. But—Harry, I—I couldn't accept—"

"The hell you can't. What choice do you have?"

She said "Oh!" and looked at him. He could see fear tightening her mouth, draining the color out from behind her faint dusting of freckles.

"Yes," Harry said, "I'm a big operator in the white slave trade. Break all my girls in personally. And do they love it!"

She stared at him. Then she smiled—really smiled.

"Forgive me," she said.

"Lord, honey, for what?"

"For thinking that. And for being as transparent as window glass. You read my mind so easily—"

"Only because it works in stereotypes," Harry said. "Now come on. Let's go get you your pad back.

"Harry—" she said.

"If I have to tell you that there're no strings, I'll begin to dislike you," Harry said. "And I'd rather not. You're a nice kid. Given time, you might even get to be human. Of course, with your background, that's hard, but I think you might make it. So let's not talk anymore for awhile. I'm tired . . ."

They started off down the boulevard in the direction of the métro. He didn't take her by the arm, so, at the second stride, Kathy drew ahead of him. At once she slowed her pace, and glanced down at his leg.

"An accident?" she said.

"You could call it that," Harry said. He was thinking that the accidentality lay in his being alive at all.

"But it wasn't," Kathy said.

"Now look, Miss Anne," Harry said. "Stop being nice to the colored help. To hell with the métro. Let's take a taxi."

"No," Kathy said. "It's too far. Why should you throw away your money? Besides, I'm not up to facing a Parisian taxi driver this morning. Are you?"

"I'm used to them," Harry said. "Took some doing, though. I worked up to it. Went to the zoo every day and patted the snakes on the head. Not all the snakes—just the cobras and the pit vipers . . ."

She smiled at him then; and again her smile was real. If there were any one thing that drew Americans living in Paris together, it was the painful necessity of having to deal with the French.

"Harry—why *are* they like that?" she said.

"History. Two thousand years of living in the best, the most fertile land in western Europe. The land all their neighbors wanted. So they had to be brave too frequently and too long. Ran out on them. No fun being told by long Charlie what *un grand peuple* they are when they *remember* what happened. That all of 'em put together didn't equal the performance of one battalion of Greeks . . ."

"But they *hate* us," Kathy said, "they hate—"

"Themselves, first. Followed by the Anglo-Saxon bloc. Followed by the rest of humanity. I understand that. Give 'em time. They're better now. Pride's coming back. They've got the A-bomb. One day they might even see how comical that is—a nation of dressmakers with nuclear weapons . . ."

"Harry, that's unkind!" she said sharply.

"I know. And unfair. Like all oversimplifications. They've got first-class scientific minds. They build good cars, the world's best military aircraft, fine computers and the rest of it. But whatever it is that makes 'em too good at designing women's clothes, spoils it. They've forgot that a nation's principal product always has to be —men."

She stared at him. Then she said it.

"Harry—you're a college graduate, aren't you?"

He looked at her, his face unsmiling.

"You want me to talk dialect, Miss Anne?" he said.

Two spots of bright, bright red showed in her cheeks.

"No. I want you to stop—baiting me, Harry. I, personally, have never been unkind to a—Negro, in my life . . ."

"Don't doubt it. You were maybe something worse . . ."

"Worse?" Kathy said.

"Yes. You were kind. Helpful. Gave away all your almost new clothes to the kitchen help. And expected them to be properly grateful. Like the Anglo-Saxons with the French."

"Oh!" Kathy said. "I suppose I was—condescending. But I didn't mean it that way. Besides, they weren't like you, Harry. Believe me they weren't!"

"Of course not. My old man's a doctor. My mother has a master's degree in education. They sent me to school in Switzerland when I was thirteen years old to stop me from playing with the kids of the kind of people who worked in your mother's kitchen. They were wrong. Should have let me play with 'em. Should have let me be a little nigger—like all the other little niggers. Better that than what I am—"

"And what are you?" Kathy said.

"An exile. A stranger. An alien. Not only here. In every country on God's green earth."

"Oh," Kathy said.

"That's the right answer to that one," Harry said. "Now come on."

They went down into the métro. Kathy told him the name of the station nearest her lodgings, so he went over to the map, and pushed the button next to the name of that station on the control board under the map. At once, a long string of purple lights came on, indicating the line they had to take. As he should have guessed, the station was in Passy. Expensive, aristocratic Passy, the *arrondissement* a girl like Kathy naturally would choose to live in. A hell of a long way from St. Germain-des-Prés, where they were now.

They sat side by side in the métro, because Harry had bought first-class tickets. Except during rush hours, there were nearly always seats vacant in the first-class cars—for which one could thank the celebrated frugality of the French, Harry supposed. They sat there without saying anything while the train rumbled through the bowels of Paris. They got off and changed trains where they had to, still without talking. Then they came up into the midmorning sunlight and walked slowly up the Avenue Foch.

Harry could see she was trembling. He knew why. For sheer cussedness, only two kinds of Parisians can outdo the taxi drivers: an *agent de police* of Corsican ancestry, and a concierge, female gender. *Une concierge,* Harry thought, can outdo the devil himself.

This one was the Passy type. Fat, carefully coiffed,

dressed impeccably in black. With a face made of Norman granite. Or floe ice. Or maybe both.

"Good day, M'sieu, Dame," she said.

Kathy reddened; that "M'sieu, Dame," was deliberate, and she knew it.

"It's still Mademoiselle, Madame Caillot," she said.

"Ah?" Madame Caillot said. "And this—gentleman?"

"A friend," Kathy said.

"Who has come to pay your rent?" Madame la Concierge said.

"Yes," Kathy said miserably.

"Ah!" Madame Caillot said. It was, Harry saw, recognized, perceived, a masterly "Ah." It circumscribed, included, encompassed a perfect knowledge of human frailty. It had everything in it except comprehension, compassion, charity. Nor did it include even a hint of merciful doubt.

"You're wrong!" Kathy said. "You mustn't think—"

"Think?" Madame Caillot said. "But what is there to think, my poor little one? Is it not rather to know? I closed my eyes to your slipping that pretty long-haired effeminate of yours into your chamber. You were at least discreet, and youth must be served, is it not so? But now I tell you that I will accept only your back rent and release to you your clothes. The chamber is no longer available. Your thirteenth *arrondissement mech* was sufficient. *Un sale nègre,* that is a little too much!"

"Ohhhh!" Kathy said.

Harry smiled.

"If the dirty money of the dirty nigger is not too disgusting for Madame's hands," he said in the effortless French he'd spoken since he was thirteen and one-half years old, "she has but to name the amount and I will remove my filthiness from her august presence. Well, Madame, how much?"

"Oh!" Madame Caillot said. "I did not know you were French, Monsieur! Your clothes—"

"Are American. And so am I. Tell me, Madame—how long did it take your hair to grow back out?"

Madame Caillot gasped.

"Forget it," Harry said. "How much?"

They stood on the *trottoir*, the sidewalk, outside the house and waited for a taxi to pass. Kathy had so much luggage that to carry it even to the nearest taxi stand was unthinkable. Kathy was crying again, very quietly, but in a kind of hurt, sick rage that was absolutely pure.

"Don't, honey," Harry said.

"She had no right!" Kathy got out between locked teeth. "She had no right at all to—"

"Who does?" Harry said. "I'm used to it. Came from south of the Mason'n Dixon line, myself, Miss Anne. Besides, bitchery is universal. And bastardy—spiritual, that is. Only two human traits that are."

"You're not used it! You couldn't be. There's no way on earth for anybody—"

"Ah!" Harry said.

She looked up at him.

"You're right," she whispered. "I lived down there all my life and it never even occurred to me to—"

"Even think about it. We're invisible. You don't even see us—as people, that is. Better like that. More comfortable. Oh, taxi!"

In the taxi, Kathy stopped crying. A look of impish mischief crossed her face.

"Harry, how did you know she'd been a collaborationist during the war?" she said.

"Looked at her. With a face like that hanging on her what else could she have been? Now relax, baby. Your troubles are over . . ."

They sat through the major miracle that getting from anywhere to anywhere else in Paris in an automobile and staying alive always is. Which was why, maybe, that it wasn't until the taxi driver—making, as usual, not the slightest gesture toward helping them drag all that luggage out of the cab, and grumbling profanely, also as usual, over the size of the tip—had dumped them out on the *trottoir* that Kathy even thought to ask Harry the question he had been dreading all the way over:

"Harry—where are you taking me?"

"My pad. Wait, Miss Anne! First place, I'm a little short, and bailing your clothes out of hock set me back. So I can't pay for a hotel room for you. Payday's not 'til Saturday night. In the meantime, I'll share a friend's pad. String-bass player in my quartet. And to put your little magnolia-scented mind entirely at ease, I won't even carry your bags up. Louis will do that. He's my concierge—and a good type. All you do is to gather up my toothbrush and shaving things, and send them down to me. As for eating, you can make out at the bar where we were this morning. I'll tell Emil to put it on the bill."

"Oh, Harry!" she wailed. "I can't let—"

"Now you just give me fifty or sixty reasonable alternatives. You can reimburse me when your old man's back gives out and he has to come home for a breather. Now come on. The joint's yours. Here's the key— incidentally, the *only* key. So you can relax, baby. Take a hot bath. Lie down. There're clean sheets in the armoire . . ."

"Harry, I can't tell you—"

"Then don't," he said. "Come on."

But she didn't send his shaving things down to him by Louis. She brought them herself. And the red tooled Morocco frame that had Fleur's picture in it.

"I—thought you—you might want this," she said.

"You thought right," Harry said.

"Harry, I'd swear I've seen—"

"Her face. You have. On the covers of *Vogue, Elle, Votre Beauté, L'Official,* and, lately, even *Jours de France* and *Paris Match.* She was the highest-paid model in Paris."

"Was?" Kathy said.

"Yes. She's dead. Of starvation, mostly. Trying to keep those interesting bones showing. Those bones the nance designers, who hate women anyhow and try to keep them as unappetizing as possible so they won't detract too much from those made-in-fagland glad rags, insist upon. Officially of pneumonia—which she caught modeling a wisp of airy nothing in front of Les Invalides on a morning that was two degrees below zero—"

"Oh," Kathy said. Then, "What was she? Japanese?"

"Vietnamese. My personal spoils of war. I found her sitting outside a heap of rubble that had been a house in Hué, and crying her little heart out for the people who were buried under the rubble. Her folks. Her Pa'n Ma, honeychile. Otherwise I'd have never met her. She wasn't the kind who hang out in soldiers' bars . . ."

"Oh," Kathy said. Then, "What was her name?"

"Mrs. Harry Forbes, in case you're interested. Née Fleur Quang Dang Hoc. She'd been educated by French nuns, so we could talk. You'd be surprised at the number of things we found to talk about. I used to call her 'Dragon Lady.'"

"And she—what did she call you?" Kathy said.

"'Night Soldier.' I liked that—especially after I found out that she thought my being blacker than seven shades of sin was interesting. 'You're more like us,' she'd say. 'Not one of the Big Monkeymen.' That's what the Viets call your tall, good-looking blond boys, you know . . ."

"After a short silence, Kathy said, 'You loved her very much, didn't you?"

"Not past tense, honey. That doesn't stop. That goes on. As long as I do, anyhow . . ."

"Harry," Kathy said suddenly, "let me keep her picture. 'Til tomorrow, anyhow—"

"Why?" Harry said.

"Don't know. To—to study that face, maybe. That beautiful face. To find out why—even though I didn't know her—it kind of haunts me . . ."

He looked at her.

"All right," he said. "I can spare the picture. Don't really need it. She's burned into me. All over. Everywhere. And she *was* beautiful. All the way through. Her heart was beautiful. Her soul. Big two-dollar words that don't mean anything anymore. Except that she sort of dug 'em up. Resurrected them. Put the meaning back. All the meaning, and then some . . ."

"Oh, Harry!" Kathy said.

Harry quoted softly. *Mais elle était du monde,*
Où les plus belles choses ont le pire destin—

Et rose, elle a vécu, comme vivent les roses
*L'espace d'un matin—**

Then he turned and walked away from Kathy, quietly, carefully, so that he almost didn't limp at all.

* But she was of this world,
  Where for the loveliest things,
  Fate reserves his cruelest blade;
  And being a rose, she lived as a rose
  One morning of sun and shade . . .
François de Malherbe: "*Consolation de Monsieur Périer sur la Mort de sa Fille.*" (Trans.: F.Y.)

Chapter
Two

It was another morning, the fourth of May, 1968, the day after the first student riots at the Sorbonne, about the fifteenth or the sixteenth of the twenty-seven mornings before J. Norton Nichols' back finally did give out, or reality caught up with him in some other fashion, and he wrote his daughter care of "Lost Souls Incorporated," which was what Harry called the American Express Office in the Place de l'Opéra. They, Harry and

Kathy, were sitting in what had already become their regular rendezvous, Emil's sidewalk café on the Boulevard St. Germain, where they'd met in the first place.

"It's not a shrine," Harry said, "like Les Deux Magots or Flore. Nobody comes here looking for F. Scott Fitzgerald's or Hemingway's ghost. Or trying to soak up inspiration through the cheeks of their asses. The coffee's drinkable and the croissants are fresh—usually. What more can you ask out of life?"

"Tell me about her," Kathy said.

Harry shifted the new clarinet case closer to the back of the chair he'd laid it on. He'd borrowed the money to buy the new instrument from Ahmad, so he didn't want some bustling tourist splattering it against the *trottoir* the first morning he'd had it. It was a good clarinet; better than the old one. He liked the tone of it very much.

"No," he said to Kathy. Like that. Flatly.

"Oh, I am sorry," Kathy said. "Reckon I'm kind of dense, sometimes. I can see that it—must hurt—to remember, I mean. Mustn't it, Harry?"

"Remembering doesn't hurt. It keeps me alive. What the hell else have I got?"

"Then—" Kathy said, "why won't you—"

"Satisfy your curiosity about what kind of a girl it was who showed no visible objection to sharing a black boy's bed?"

Kathy looked at him.

"Harry," she said, "I've been here nearly two years now—"

"Meaning?"

"That I've known quite a few girls—Southern girls, even—"

"I'd say especially Southern girls," Harry said. "Go on, honeychile—"

"Who not only showed no visible objection, but were—"

"Disgustingly eager—" Harry supplied.

"All right! Who were disgustingly eager to try it! And don't sit there looking at me out of the corner of your eyes like a sleek black cat just because I can't shed my background like a torn nightie! I wish I could, but I can't. In fact, if I were a Negro, I'd find the attentions of those girls insulting."

"I did," Harry said. "I do. The ultimate rebellion. They lie there and get even with papa. Or with hubby. Achieve even orgasm through anger. Which reduces their black partners to artificial penises, like in the Manners' Experiment. And love, or at least coitus, to mutual masturbation. Which is why this little black downhome boy bowed out. A long time ago. Learned to say 'No'—politely."

Kathy looked at him. Really looked at him.

"I suppose you have had your share of invitations," she said slowly. "Even with my background I can see you're awf'ly good-looking . . ."

"Why, thanks, Miss Anne," Harry said.

"Don't be sarcastic! I mean it. In spite of your color, you're—"

"Now just you hold on one minute, honeychile. If I have any looks at all—an item I've never wasted two consecutive seconds thinking about in my life—it's *because* I'm black, not in spite of it. Just as your freckles, green eyes, and blond hair don't hurt you, any. Good Lord, I'm dead beat, and you make me waste my whole morning educating you. All right—I'll leave you one to chew on before I hit the hay. Ever hear the story of the African king and the bathing beauty?"

"No," Kathy said. "Tell me."

"True story. Really happened. German girl—perfect Aryan Nordic type—whatever the hell that means. Miss Europe, circa 1932. Flying over the jungle when her plane crashed. The pygmies found her and tried to sell her to an Ibo tribal king. No deal. Wouldn't buy. Said to the pygmies: 'What kind of jackass do you take me for? Trying to sell me this freak. No tits, no tail, and somebody's peeled all the skin off her! Bug off with her, you little buggers!' "

"So?" Kathy said.

"So when you get to the place that you see the Ibo king was perfectly right, or at least perfectly entitled to his opinions, you'll be getting there, Miss Anne. Now, good-bye. I need sleep. Tooting a clarinet in an all-night joint doesn't leave a guy feeling like the power and the glory, you know . . ."

"Harry—" she said.

"Yes, Kathy?"

"Don't go yet. I need company. I'm all alone and scared and—and I've got to tell you something. It—it's unfair not to—"

"Spill it, then," Harry said.

"No. I can't. Not yet, I mean. Later on I will. Later on I'll have to. Just—talk to me. Tell me about—Fleur. She *was* in love with you, wasn't she, Harry?"

"Jesus H. Christ!" Harry said.

"Oh, I am sor—"

"You can take that sorrow and shove it," Harry said. "Look, Miss Anne. I don't know whether Fleur was in love with me or not. What man *knows* that about what woman—even after he's been married to her for forty years and she's given him eighteen kids? All I know is what she did—"

"And what did she do?" Kathy said.

"Kept me for three months. I couldn't find a job here. Not without papers, you understand. So she worked like a dog—no, like a nigger—at that miserable modeling racket, and brought me home every sou she'd made. Came home reeling on her feet, beat, done in, whipped, and insisted on cooking me something hot— usually one of those crazy Vietnamese dishes—before going to bed. She even got me the job I still have, through an Algerian girl who worked with her. Kid who was sleeping with Zahibuine . . ."

"Zahibuine?" Kathy said. "Seems to me I've heard, or read—"

"Read. Ahmad is always in the papers, usually because somebody's tried to kill him. Again. Good type, Ahmad. Only his little friends do play rough."

"She was in love with you, then," Kathy said. "She was brought up without prejudices—"

Harry grinned suddenly.

"Oh, she had her prejudices all right," he said. "Couldn't stand your 'Big Monkeymen.' Claimed that their smell made her toss her cookies."

"Harry—"

"I'm not kidding. She did. Sometimes I think that's what makes anybody with one drop of English blood in their veins invincible—that absolute inability to see the other fellow's point of view."

"Harry, I'm perfectly capable—"

"No, you're not. If I were to tell you that Fleur was proud of me, that she used to drag me around to show me off to her girl friends, you'd have a hard time keeping your face straight—"

"I would not! I told you before, I can see you're awfully good-looking . . ."

"Thanks again," Harry said. "Come on now, spill it. Whatever it is that's exercising your little pink tripes, I mean. Tell ol' Uncle Harry—"

"Harry, sometimes you make me so mad I could spit! Half the time I don't know whether you're brainwashing me or using me to get even with the whole white race—"

Harry grinned at her.

"Or both, or neither. You figure it out, Miss Anne," he said.

"Stop calling me 'Miss Anne,' damnit! Oh, Harry, I—" Then, abruptly, she bent her head and started to cry.

He put out his hand and caught her chin between his strong, agile, musician's fingers; lifted her head effortlessly until she was facing him. Said:

"Don't, Kathy." Like that. Very gently.

"All right," she whispered. "You're good. Too good to lie to, anyhow. I—I think—I'm—oh, Harry—my period's three weeks overdue and this morning I threw up and—"

He sat there. Then he said:

"Your rent was *two* months overdue, Kathy."

"I know! I know! But I loaned him the money I was supposed to pay the rent with the first time. And after that, when I wouldn't let him have anymore, he—"

"Stole the second month's. I see. Figures."

"Harry, don't look at me like that! I'm not a tramp! I—"

"I know," Harry said. "Tramps don't get caught. It's

the sweet innocents who don't know what a diaphragm's for, or where to buy *la pilule,* who do. All right. Do I find you an abortionist or would you rather have Lover Boy back?"

Her head came up. She shook it very slowly from side to side. The sun slanted across the boulevard and illuminated her tears. The funny part about it was they had soot in them. Tears in Paris nearly always do.

"Neither," she said.

"Neither?" Harry said.

"I—couldn't kill my baby. I mean to spend the rest of my life making up to him—"

"Or her—" Harry said.

"Or her—and I do hope it *is* a her!—for the father I wished off on her. That's not the problem."

"Then what *is* the problem?" Harry said.

"I—I can't go home like this. What on earth could I tell Papa?"

"Like the Indian maid: 'How!' Then Big Chief Papa says: 'Me know *how*. Who?' "

"Oh, Jesus, Harry! People have been murdered for better jokes than that! But I still don't see what—"

"On earth you can tell Papa. Leave it to me, baby. I'll figure out something . . ."

Then the idea came to him—for the first time. *How* he could save this gilded waif. The absolutely perfect— or the perfectly appalling—stratagem. He couldn't decide which it was, or anything else about it except that it was curiously appealing in ways that his sure self-knowledge told him were rooted in the habituated victim's too easy acceptance of his enemy's image of him, and hence bordered on masochism. He thought, "Why in God's unholy name should I? This poor bedraggled little honky bitch with half a brain and that half-lame and yet I—"

He said, "Go home. Get some sleep. Meet me here tomorrow and I—"

"Harry, tomorrow's ten thousand years from now! I'll go crazy, lying there thinking. Couldn't I come to your club tonight—and listen to you play? Then afterwards we—"

"No," he said.

His tone made her stare at him.

"Why not?" she whispered.

"Wouldn't want to see you shot or dismembered by a satchel charge of plastic or—"

"Harry! You work at that place that they—"

"Shot up a couple of weeks back. Yes. And before that they plasticized the Ladies' john. Blew the bidet clear across the street."

"Oh, Harry! Why on earth don't you—"

"Quit? Say I prefer being shredded to starving to death. I've got papers to work in Ahmad's *boîte*. And papers, *ma cherie*, are papers. Now scat. Go home. Lie down. Take care of *l'enfant de la patrie*, will you? After all, it's not *his* fault."

"Hers. It's going to be a girl. It has to be."

"And *why* has it to be, honeychile?" Harry said.

"Because I couldn't stand it if it were a boy. A boy would turn out to be just like *him*, likely. While a girl—"

"Would naturally take after her mother? I see. Big deal."

She looked at him and her eyes were very wide and focused on nothing. Then they went absolutely blind and her chin quivered like an idiot child's. She put both her hands to her middle as though he'd hit her in the belly with his fist.

"Kathy—" he said.

"You're right," she whispered. "If it's a boy, it'll be a pimp and a thief, and if it's a girl, it'll be a whore. That's what you meant, wasn't it?"

"No," he said mercilessly. "Whores get paid."

"Oh, Jesus!" Kathy said.

"Now I'm sorry," Harry said, "truly."

She shook her head.

"No, you're not. What you are is even—with this one poor representative of the white race, anyhow. All right, I'm down. All the way down. Go on, step on me. That was what you were trying to do, wasn't it? Kill what little self-respect I have left? Well, you—you've done it. Now how do you feel? Happy? Proud?"

"Rotten," he said quietly. Then, "I suppose you're right. I suppose there was something like that in the back part of my mind. Only it wasn't conscious. Believe me it wasn't, Kathy. And I am sorry. Forgive me, won't you?"

She turned away from him and looked down the boulevard.

"For what?" she said. "For making me see what I am? A—a pushover. The girl with the ball-bearing heels. All right. So what do I do next? Start sleeping with *you*?"

"No," he said. "Told you I was choicy. Oh hell! Let's quit this, shall we? Why should we fight? You're at rock bottom, and I'd have to climb up through twenty tons of shit'n gravel to even get to where you are now. A truce, huh? Long enough to figure a way to get you out of the mess you're in?"

"Why should you?" she said tonelessly.

"Don't know. To make up for that streak of nigger-mean I just showed you, maybe . . ."

"Forget it. I had it coming, I guess. Harry—are abortions—dangerous?"

"They sure as hell *are*. And the types who do them are a sight lower than a maggot's belly. The outcasts of the medical profession. Most of 'em on pot, or something worse. The mortality rate's twenty times what it is in countries where it's legal to do them."

"What countries?" she said.

"Sweden, for one. Had the money, I'd take you there. Now there's a thought! Maybe I could put another touch on Ahmad—sell him a bill of goods—"

"What bill of goods?" Kathy said.

"Like, say, your boy's in the Army. You're married to him, see. And we have to drop the package before he gets back—"

"We?" Kathy said. "You'd assume responsibility?"

"Why not? Ahmad would believe me. He's always kidding me about my cheering section. All the little girls with the long, lank hairdos, horn-rimmed spectacles, chewed-off fingernails, and dirty feet, who come to listen to me toot the pipe. He'd be glad to help me out. He'd think I'd finally taken his advice—"

"What advice?" Kathy whispered.

"To stop moping over Fleur. To find a substitute for her. Fat chance. Anyhow, it's worth a try. Tonight, I'll—"

"No," Kathy said.

"Why not?" Harry said.

"It—my baby's—alive. I know, I know! Right now, it's

only a little pink bunch of cells you'd need a microscope to even find, but all the same—"

"It's the start of—a man. Or a woman. A being called human. Having what the ecclesiastical authorities call an immortal soul. Never could buy that bit. Once asked old Prof Heimer—Physics One—he was my favorite among all my teachers, to define the soul. Looked at me over the top of his specs and said in that slow, dry way he had: 'A semantic irrelevancy, Forbes!' "

"You said—your Fleur had one. A soul, I mean."

"*She* did. But then she was a human being. No if's, and's, or but's about it. Indisputably. So nothing about her was irrelevant. You see?"

"No, I don't see. The way you say that, anybody would think *I'm* not human, or at least that you don't think I am—"

"You're not. Me neither. The exact second you stop thinking about everything in terms of first-person singular, and starting every sentence with a capital 'I,' you'll begin to get there, Miss Anne—"

"And you," she said, looking at him, her eyes bleak, her mouth bitter. "What'll *you* have to do to get there, Harry?"

"Stop confusing your nice little shape with the map of Georgia. Quit heaping coals of fire on your head. 'Cause vengeance ain't nobody's, honeychile, not even the Lord's. Slimiest kind of perversion there is, I reckon."

She went on looking at him.

"Do you have *that* much to get even for?" she said.

"I lived nineteen million years in Georgia," Harry said quietly, "before I got out."

"Meaning you were nineteen years old when you lcft?" Kathy said.

"You could put it that way. My slant is that anywhere in the United States of America a black boy's *born* a million years old. And that he keeps aging a thousand years a minute as long as he lives. That is, if he stays alive. And if you can call what he does living—"

She considered that. For approximately thirty seconds. Which was, after all, a respectable enough length of time for a girl in her present circumstances to consider a problem which didn't directly concern her, Harry thought. Only it did concern her—and directly. Because it was going to shape, or more likely distort, what was going to happen to her next.

" 'No man is an island,' " he said.

"What did you say?" Kathy said.

"Nothing," Harry said. "Go home, Kathy. Lie down. Tomorrow—"

"No," she said. "What you're going to tell me to-morrow you've already thought up now. I know you that well, Harry. You're quick. Your mind works fast. Fast and weird."

"I'm a disciple of Ionesco, Beckett *et cie*," Harry said. "I believe in absurdity—"

"Tell me!" Kathy said.

"All right. You go home to Pops with a license to commit maternity. Signed, sealed, and delivered with his blessing by the mayor at *la Mairie*—which you explain to Pops means City Hall. So grandson will be legal—thus sharply limiting the amount of screaming Pops can do. Friend hubby will *not* be among those present. You've made a mistake, for which you're properly sorry. But you don't mean to spend the rest of your life with—

what is it that Pops cottons to least? A dope addict? A lush? A nance? A double-gaited nance, of course, but—"

"Harry—" Kathy said.

"Let me finish. At the proper intervals prescribed by French law, you'll get letters—in French—demanding that you return to friend hubby's bed and board. After six months of silence on your part, or better still, a bitter and indignant refusal from you, hubby then divorces you. A copy of which bill of divorcement will in due course be delivered you. Then you marry some nice Robert E. Reb, and you, he, and *l'enfant de la patrie* live happily forever after. All right?"

"No. Not all right. Who on earth could you find that you can trust that much? That I—" She stopped short, stared at him. When she spoke again, her voice had horror in it; the thing, itself, not the sound of it.

"No. Oh, no!" she said.

"In name only," he said quietly. "I'm not hard up, Miss Anne. Besides that bit about all cats being gray in the dark is way off. Say, tame Angoras with pink ribbons 'round their necks bore me—"

"*White* Angoras—" she said.

"I'll admit to a certain amount of reciprocal prejudice," Harry said. "But mainly it's the voice of experience putting its two sous' worth in. All factors being duly considered, nothing beats a little jungle voodoo in the hay. Certainly not a northern fjord—or a London fog. I chill easy."

She was staring at him now. Hard.

"Harry," she said, "why do you hate me so?"

"Lord God!" Harry said.

"You do. From the first, you—you've taken advantage of me. Oh, not in the usual ways. You're too smart for that—too subtle. You knew from the outset I wouldn't —wrong word—say, couldn't. That's truer and less— insulting. You knew from the outset I *couldn't* go to bed with you, so you've been killing me little by little— with kindness. With the unkindest kind of kindness in the world . . ."

"No. You don't read me, honeychile. It's more like a line out of Omar—or Fitzgerald. The one about smashing this sorry scheme of things entire—"

"In order to rebuild it nearer to your heart's desire? No, Harry. You can't. I'm not your Fleur. And I couldn't be. You ought to know that—"

"Right," Harry said. "That takes too long. Took even her a few million years . . ."

"A few *million* years?" Kathy said.

"Yes. To get to be her. To dream herself into being. To create—perfection. Sitting there beside a lotus pool, all that time, dreaming. Or beside the Perfumed River. Funny thing—it stinks like hell, that river . . ."

"Oh, damnit!" Kathy said. "You're impossible to talk to!"

"I'm impossible, period. You ought to ask my Ma sometime. She caught me in a riverfront whorehouse when I was twelve years old. That's why she made the old man ship me off to Switzerland . . ."

"Har—ry—"

"Fact. Know what I was doing there?"

"No, and I don't want to! Why—"

"Playing piano. Getting in some real hot licks. Made the joint rock. Of course they paid me, but it wasn't the dough. It was that big fat beautiful chance to do what I wanted to. What I was born to do. The girls used to sit around—between customers, that is—and listen to me beat the hell out of that old wreck. Which reminds me. Did I ever tell you the story of my life?"

"No. And you're not, now. What fun do you get out of lying to me, Harry?"

He looked at her, solemnly.

"None," he said, "which is why I don't."

"Harry," she said, slowly, pushing the words out on little, ragged pulsations of breath, "what *am* I going to do?"

He went on looking at her, a long, slow time.

"Accept my offer," he said.

"But, Harry, I—"

"Accept it," he said. "And spend the rest of your life living with its consequences. Wait! Those consequences are really rough. A debt you *can't* pay back. Owing your future to a guy with the wrong camouflage job. Remembering that he never so much as touched your little finger. Struggling with the suspicion that he didn't even want to, maybe. And wondering why . . ."

"I know why," she said bitterly. "You don't even *see* me. I'm just a—an object to you. A kind of a scapegoat you use to—"

He smiled at her then.

"That being so, what've you got to worry about, Miss Anne?" he said.

Her head came up. That look which was the thing he liked most of all about her, that flare and flash of nerve-naked pride, that quality she had he could only debase by calling sheer guts—which it was, of course; but also something else, something more—was back in her eyes.

"Nothing!" she said. "All right. I become Mrs. Harry Forbes. The Second Mrs. Harry Forbes. Temporarily. But I'm warning you, Harry. If you ever so much as—

touch me, try to kiss me, say—I—I'll kill you! So help me, I'll—"

He stood there looking at her. A long time. A very long time.

"You kept Fleur's picture two nights, Kathy," he said. "Told me you wanted to study it. But you didn't even learn the first lesson—"

"Which was?" she said.

"That the kind of a guy who'd go for her *wouldn't* go for you, maybe. That it's mighty goddamned hard to find an even acceptable substitute for perfection, let alone a replacement. That you, baby—blonde hair, blue eyes, and all—just ain't in Fleur's league. And the only reason I don't explain what I mean even better is that it gripes my big gut to mention her name and yours in the same breath . . ."

He turned then and started off, away from her, down the street. For once, his limp was marked. But she came racing after him, took his arm.

"Harry," she said, "I *am* sorry. Believe me, I am."

"All right," he said, tiredly. Then he grinned. "You just solved one problem, anyhow—"

"What problem?" Kathy said.

"What to give you for a wedding present. A thirty-eight. Gold-plated. And with pearl handles. Like that dame in that picture two, three years ago . . ."

"Harry, you can't do this. I can't accept it. Besides, why should you?"

"No reason. Because it makes no sense, which makes it right. A part of the pattern of the universe. My two-bit contribution to the galloping insanity the world's dying of. A nice, fat, assbackwards bit of absurdity. Because making sense has been banned these days, Kathy.

Unlawful. Or immoral. Or both. I wouldn't know—"

"Harry," she said sadly, "now I *have* hurt your feelings, haven't I?"

He considered that.

"No," he said. "Say, rather, you've disappointed me, a little—"

"Disappointed you how?"

"Kicked the hell out of one of my pet theories—that even upper-class white Southerners are human beings. Or can be taught to be. That the material's there. A minimum residue of decency, say. Or even enough plain damned common sense to realize that the excess pigmentation of my hide, or the lack of it in yours, doesn't matter a good goddamn in the scale of things. Seems I was wrong. You really are hopeless, aren't you?"

She bowed her head.

"Yes," she said, "I am. But not for the reasons you think. Harry, for a person as smart as you are, you really are awfully stupid, you know . . ."

He grinned at her happily.

"*Now* we're getting somewhere," he said. "Would you care to elucidate, Miss Anne?"

"Explain, not elucidate. You've the damnedest habit of using overblown language, Harry. I know you're educated. In fact, just from listening to you, I'll bet you graduated with honors—cum laude, likely."

"Summa," Harry said, "and with a letter in track, to boot. Which doesn't prove I was smart. All it proves is that I was driven. So—"

"So if you know that much, you ought to realize a couple of other things. You *can't* prove anything to me, Harry. Or to anybody, for that matter. You can't. Nobody can. It's impossible. You think I don't *know* this race business is nonsense? You believe I can't *see* which of the two of us is the better human being? Don't you even give me credit for having enough brains to be able to tell the difference between a—a slut and—and a poet, sort of?"

"So?" Harry said, again.

"Only Harry, Harry—who ever told you that what a person knows has anything to do with what a person feels?"

He stood there, studying her. Nodded, slowly.

"There you have me, Kathy," he said.

She looked down, looked up again. He saw the tears haze her eyes over suddenly.

"There I don't have you," she said. "And I never can. Would you believe that I'm—ashamed of that, Harry? I am. Only my being ashamed doesn't help anything, either—Harry—?"

"Yes, Kathy?"

"Let me come to your club tonight. It isn't very likely that M'sieu Zahibuine's enemies will—"

He thought about that.

"I don't suppose they'll pull another fast one soon," he said. "Besides, Ahmad's spread the word that he's selling the joint. He has to. People don't cotton to the idea of being perforated or shredded as a part of the evening's entertainment. So we're playing to empty tables every night. All right. I'll reserve a place for you. You're coming alone, or you want to bring a friend?"

"I don't have any friends—except you. That is, if you *are*. I doubt it, sometimes. Besides—"

"Besides what?" Harry said.

"It wouldn't look right. For—your fiancée to show up with somebody else. Now would it, Harry?"

He saw a flash of that pure gamine's mischief—another thing about her that was beginning to get to him—light her eyes.

He grinned back at her.

"I'd break his backbone for him if you did," he said. " 'Til tonight, then, Kathy—"

She did a strange thing then. She went up on tiptoe and kissed his cheek. A light, brushing kiss that almost didn't touch. Then she saw his eyes.

"Oh, Harry, I am sor—" she began.

"Don't ever do that again," he said, too quietly. "Not ever, as long as you live."

Then he turned and limped away from her, down the crowded street.

Chapter
Three

When Kathy Nichols came into Le Blue Note, Fats Winkler, the string-bass player, was taking a solo. He curved his immense, yellow-skinned, sweaty bulk around the big viol like a lover, and made black magic, evoking Africa, night, love, and pain in one long, unbroken, endlessly elaborated, atonal line. His pudgy fingers moved over the strings powerfully. He had his eyes more than half-closed, which made his moon-shaped face the perfect image of a Buddha, lost in some contemplative ecstasy.

"That's her?" he said to Harry without changing his expression or missing a beat. "That there's your gray chick, boy?"

"Yes," Harry said.

"Mighty fine," Fats said. "Mighty fine. How come you ain't layin' her, Harry? You gone crazy or something?"

"Maybe I've switched over," Harry said. "Started working the other side of the street—"

"Shit," Fats said. "Don't hand me that crap, Harry. Know you too well. You ain't got a queer bone in your lil' ol' charcoal blond body. Hell, you don't even have to hustle up a piece no more. Every night they're outside, lined up, their door keys in their hands—"

"Cool it, Fats," Harry said.

Fats finished his stint and bowed. Big as he was, his every movement was graceful. A wave of applause came up from the tables. Either the customers believe Ahmad's lies about selling this joint, or their memories are piss-poor, Harry thought.

Fats was staring at Kathy.

"Downhome where I come from," he groaned, "we'd call that table tail, and you—"

"She's holding out for the license," Harry said. "They brought her up strict, downhome . . ."

Fats looked at him.

"And you're weakening," he said. "Tell Buzz to take a riff. Gonna talk to that lil' girl . . ."

"Fats!" Harry said, sharply.

"Don't you worry none, soul brother!" Fats said. "Gonna be on my best behavior. Sweet-talk her a little, see where she's at. 'Cause of all the ways of breaking your hump, getting mixed up with gray chicks longer than two nights in a row is the worst. You hear me talkin' to you, man?"

Then he was gone, down from the bandstand. He wafted his way among the tables like a balloon on a low tether, carrying his two hundred and twenty pounds as though they were so many ounces.

He pulled up a chair and sat down without saying a word to Kathy. Then he put his elbows on the table, cradled his round face in his fat hands, and silently stared at her.

"I—I'm sure I don't know—" Kathy faltered.

"But you will, girl friend," Fats said. "Gonna be Harry's best man. That is, if you get by me."

"Get by you?" Kathy got out. "I'm afraid I don't understand, Mister—"

"Fats to you, girl baby. Harry's my friend. And he's had a rough go. You know about Fleur?"

"Yes," Kathy said.

"Hurt him. Losing Fleur, I mean. Hurt him real bad. Right now he's in no shape for another shitty deal. You read me, girl baby?"

Kathy smiled. But her voice, speaking, tightened up on her. Lost its drawl. Came over with a reedy edge to it. Still, all things considered, her control was admirable.

"You think poor Harry needs protection from this designing woman?" she said.

Fats stared at her.

"No," he said slowly. "Designs he'd see through before you'd got 'em half figured out yourself, girl baby. Harry's smart—"

"Then?" Kathy said.

"Needs protection from—himself," Fats said. "Good-hearted boy, Harry. Always giving folks the benefit of the doubt. Fleur's fault, in a way. Left him believing people's mostly good—"

"While you believe they're mostly bad?" Kathy said.

"Hell, no. Being bad takes more grit'n ginger than most people's got in 'em. What folks are, baby, are a bunch of weak polecats who can't stand their own stink. What I'm trying to figure is what he sees in you—besides all that first-class equipment you're sitting on and poking my eyes out with, I mean . . ."

"Why, thank you, Fats!" Kathy said. "I think you're just darling, too!"

"Don't be sarcastic, girl baby. Was me, wouldn't be no sweat. I wouldn't see or be interested in anything else. But then Fleur convinced him that women is people. A mistake, mostly."

"You mean you think we *aren't?*" Kathy bristled. "Why—"

"Hold on, girl friend. Know you *are*. My Ma was people. The greatest. The mistake is *treating* you like people. Don't think there's a girlchild born what don't quit lovin' a man the exact second she quits being scared of him—at least a little . . ."

"Then Harry—has nothing to worry about," Kathy whispered. "He—terrifies me . . ."

Fats stared at her.

"That's going a little too far," he said. "Tell me something, girl baby. You're for real? You love Harry?"

Kathy stared down at her hands. Then she looked up again. But she didn't lie. She knew the quality of her adversary now.

"No," she said. "I—I admire him immensely, Fats, but—"

Fats studied her face, her eyes. Loosed an almost soundless little whistle.

"Thought y'all had the fiddlers tuning up that crazy bit from *Lohengrin*," he said.

"Yes—" Kathy said, "but—"

"But you're marrying him for reasons," Fats said. "Reasons what don't include love. Only now, he's got you running scared. Give him time. He'll have you listening to your heart instead of your head. He's gifted that way. And he can pick 'em, usually—"

"Except that now you think he's made a mistake, don't you, Fats?" Kathy said.

"No. I think *you* have," Fats said. "Buy you a drink, girl friend?"

"Oh—all right. Just a lemonade, though. Nothing strong—"

"You name your poison, girl baby. But you mean to tell me that all the time you've been holding hands with Harry you don't know him any better than *that*?"

"I—I don't understand you, Fats. I—"

"Item one, he ain't hard up. Got so many dames he shares the leftovers with the band. Item two, he don't fight dirty. Don't have to. Why should a guy who can pull a snow job the way he can have to waste time lushing a babe up?"

"It's not that!" Kathy said sharply. "I don't drink because I can't. I get weepy. Two stiff ones and I start crying in my cups. That's the only reason. I—I trust Harry. He's proved to me I can—"

Fats grinned at her, then.

"So now the worry is—can you trust *you?* Eh, girl baby?" he said.

He saw the startled leap of her eyes. Then they turned inward, gazing in upon—not recognition, surely. She hadn't gotten that far, yet. But a quality that was one remove from it: the awareness that undreamed of, unimaginable possibilities exist, even in one's own psyche, once one had wandered far from hearth and tribe.

Fats sat there. It was her problem. He had a decided weakness for good-looking young women of any hue, but he armored his heart against this one. His sure instinct warned him she was dangerous.

"Oh!" Kathy said, "I—"

"Forget it," Fats said. "Gar—song, *un citron pressé, s'il vous plaît!*"

But when the waiter came back he didn't bring lemonade. He brought a floor stand and put a silver ice bucket on top of it. In the bucket was champagne. A whole magnum. Piper Heidseck, '47.

"Compliments of M'sieu Ahmad," the waiter said. "And he has given orders that anything Mademoiselle wishes is to be provided her—on the house. If Mademoiselle is hungry, I should be happy to suggest—"

"No, thank you," Kathy whispered. "Later, perhaps—"

"You speak French *good,*" Fats said approvingly.

"Fats—" Kathy said.

"Yes, baby girl?"

"Tell me about—her," Kathy said.

"Fleur?" Fats said.

"Yes," Kathy said.

"Big order, baby. The closest I can get to that would

be to say that if I was a dame, I sure would hate like hell to have to follow—Fleur."

"Oh," Kathy said.

"She was a little thing. Tiny. Knee-high to a grasshopper. But—perfect. Like a lil' statue carved out of old ivory. Her voice tinkled. Triads. Three notes, y'know—like one of them crazy three-string Chinese guitars. The morning after I met her I was on my way to the Embassy to sign up for Vietnam—see if I could find me one just like her. They wouldn't take me. Too damn' fat."

"You mean—you were in love with her, too?"

"Yep. Sure Lord was. Me 'n every other man who ever laid eyes on her. But she couldn't see nobody else but Harry. Baby, I sure hope you know what you're doing, 'cause any guy who's been loved like that is purely ruint for life!"

"Oh," Kathy said, "She—she loved him *that* much?"

"He'd come into the house, and the minute he sat down, she'd be on her knees, tugging at his shoelaces, with his slippers already ready. Used to embarrass the hell out of him at first. Other lil' tricks, too—like hot perfumed towels on his forehead when he was resting. Sitting on his knees and feeding him things, and laughing—in triads. Damnit, I could see 'em! The notes was silver. When she was happy, anyhow. When she was sad, they was bronze colored . . ."

"Was she sad often?" Kathy said.

"Well—yes. Towards the end. After Harry'd got to be famous and acquired his cheering section. Some of those babes weren't hard on the eye and they could be persistent as all hell—"

"Did he—did Harry give her reasons to be—"

"Jealous? No. Never looked at another dame. Only she thought that because they were Europeans they were maybe prettier than her—"

"And were they? Some of them, anyhow?"

"Baby girl, I'm prejudiced," Fats said. "Far as I'm concerned, nobody could be prettier'n Fleur. Now I got to get back to work. Tell you one thing, though. You come close. First babe I've met who does. Maybe that's why you get to Harry—"

"Thanks," Kathy said. "Fats, ask Harry to play something for me, will you?"

"I'll do that little old thing," Fats said. "Bye now, babydoll—"

Kathy sipped her champagne. The bubbles in it tickled her nose. Her hand, holding the champagne glass, shook. She tried to stop it, but she couldn't. She gripped the glass so tight that the stem of it broke, and the jagged edges of it cut her hand. She sat there, staring at the broken goblet, at the champagne on the table, at the red of her own blood that was flooding out of her hand. She felt sick. She thought, I mustn't faint. I mustn't!

By that time, both the waiter, and another man she had never seen before, were there.

"Mademoiselle!" the waiter said. "But you are wounded! How—"

"*Ta gueule!*" the other man said sharply, leaving Kathy, sick as she really was, to reflect with admiration on how many things you could say in French that you can't in any other language, so that Ahmad Zahibuine— it has to be, she thought, it can't be anybody else—had only to say *"Ta gueule!"* for the waiter to get it all: "Will you please be so kind as to shut your muzzle of a braying ass and let me think?" or words to that effect.

"Go into my office," Ahmad said. "In the top left-hand drawer of my desk, there is a first-aid kit. Here is the key. March yourself, Jean Claude!"

Then he was sitting at the table and wrapping a napkin around Kathy's cut hand. She looked up then and saw Harry standing beside the table.

"Kathy," he said, and the pain in his voice was real.

"I'm all right, Harry," she said. "M'sieu Zahibuine is taking very good care of me." Then she added, in French, "Is it not so, M'sieu Zahibuine?"

"The best," Ahmad said pleasantly. "Do not preoccupy yourself, Harry. Go back to the bandstand and make us beautiful music. And Harry—"

"Yes, Ahmad?" Harry said.

"I felicitate you. She is *really* something. Every happiness, *mon brave!*"

Harry stood there. But there was no mockery in Ahmad's voice.

"Please, Harry," Kathy said. "Everybody's looking at us. Go play something *special* for me, will you—please?"

"D'accord," Harry said shortly, and left them there.

But before Kathy could say anything to Ahmad, a fat blond man who had the aspect of a well-scrubbed Normandy pig was bowing over the table.

"I am a physician," he said. "Will you have the goodness to let me see your hand, Mademoiselle?"

Ahmad took the napkin off. The blood came flooding out. Kathy turned her face away, shuddering.

"Tiens!" the fat doctor said. "Not good. Not good at

all. You will make a tourniquet, M'sieu. Here, about the wrist, with another napkin. Meanwhile I will go to my car *chercher mon sac.*"

"Thank you, Doctor," Ahmad said.

"*De rien,*" the doctor said.

Ahmad ripped another napkin into strips, wrapped the longest strip around Kathy's wrist, and jerked it tight. The bleeding slowed, but it didn't stop. Ahmad frowned, worriedly.

"Do you perhaps have hemophilia?" he said, and smiled. "It is not too rare in those of royal blood—"

"But I haven't any royal blood," Kathy said.

"To be sure you have! You're a princess, at least. A beautiful princess sleeping in her tower until the black knight—"

"Ahmad—M'sieu Zahibuine—please!" Kathy said.

"Ah?" Ahmad said.

"Forgive me," Kathy said. "I'm a little sick and all confused and—" Then she blurted it out, what she'd been thinking from the moment she saw him, this tall, exceedingly good-looking man whose skin was tan, but no darker than that of many Spaniards or Italians— "Are you married, M'sieu Zahibuine?"

Ahmad laughed merrily.

"Too much so," he said. "I have one nice, fat wife who is of the race of Harry, though not quite so black. I am also the father of eight children—" he paused, and added slowly, "at home—"

"*Chez vous?*" Kathy repeated a little stupidly; then she got it. "And—away from home, M'sieu Zahibuine?"

"Allah in His wisdom only knows," Ahmad said. "Ah, here is our friend, M'sieu le Medicin! And Jean Claude with the first-aid kit, finally, now that we no longer need it, of course!"

"Could we not retire to your office, M'sieu?" the doctor said. "It will be necessary to take stitches in this pretty little hand. I am afraid, Mademoiselle, that it is going to hurt. But you will be brave, will you not, my poor little one?"

"Yes," Kathy whispered. "Yes, Doctor, I will be brave . . ."

When it was over, when the fat little doctor had cleaned the slivers of glass out of that nasty cut and had taken three stitches in it, refusing, indignantly, Ahmad's offer to pay him, Kathy and her host came back to the table. Kathy could see Harry looking at her. Somehow, in a way she didn't understand, that gave her a feeling of triumph. Besides, she really had been brave.

"You will now," Ahmad Zahibuine said firmly, "drink three glasses of champagne, one after another, very fast. Without squeezing them, of course."

Kathy laughed.

"And, after that," Ahmad said, "you will tell me why you wanted to know whether I was married or not. Is it that you wish to marry me?"

"Oh!" Kathy faltered, "I—"

"You are supposed to marry Harry, who is black. And, it seems to me, you are confused about the matter—"

Kathy looked at him. Decided at once that she could trust him.

"You have reason, M'sieu Zahibuine. I *am* confused. I admire Harry tremendously, but—"

"You do not love him." It was a statement, not a question.

"No," Kathy said, "I do not love him. I am—I am—*sudiste*—a Southerner, you understand, M'sieu—"

"Call me Ahmad," Zahibuine said.

"Ahmad. For me, for any white girl of my background, the idea that she could even drift—as I seem to have—into any sort of personal relationship with a black man —is almost beyond imagination. It's hard to change the ways one was brought up to accept. Is it that you comprehend this, Ahmad?"

"No," Ahmad said. "Is it that you have the *préjugés raciales?*"

"No!" Kathy said. "I don't! I have never had. That is what is perhaps the strangest of all. I don't dislike black people. I've always been rather fond of them—"

"In the same fashion," Ahmad said sadly, "that a certain type of romantic Englishman, who fancies himself a new Lawrence of Arabia, is fond of the Arab . . ."

Kathy looked at him.

"I'm afraid I don't understand that, Ahmad."

"Drink your champagne, Kathy. My pretty Kathy who very probably doesn't understand anything. Stay that way. It is better for you."

Tears of pure exasperation stung Kathy's eyes.

"That's the main thing I have against Harry," she said. "He treats me always the way you're doing now, as though I were a child or a fool—"

"Or both. In some ways, both," Ahmad said gently. "Another word for it is—innocence. Keep that quality, Kathy. It becomes you . . ."

"I'm not innocent!" Kathy said angrily. "I—"

"You mean you have gone to bed with men. Though not with Harry—of that I am sure."

"Why are you so sure?" Kathy said.

"Because you would not be able to maintain your present attitude towards him. I have known several of his little friends. And not one of them was the same afterwards. Harry may be many things, *mais, comme homme, il est quelque chose de sérieux* . . ."

In English, the phrase "As a man, he is something serious" doesn't mean anything definite; but in French, it does. She knew what it meant. And it was one of the things that made her afraid. She felt a certain surge of panic, as though they—Fats, Ahmad, the world—were tightening a noose about her neck. A noose that simultaneously bound her to Harry—to that—nigger, she thought viciously, and sat there, trembling with both shock and shame. It was a word, an epithet she had never consciously employed before in her life. Not even in thought. People of her social class never do. They say "Negro" too carefully.

And it was then, at that precise moment, that Harry began to play. Of course, he'd been playing before. All evening, in fact. But not like—this. He stood up suddenly, a thing he almost never did because of his bad leg—and slanted the clarinet out and down. His long, slim, powerful fingers dug into the keys, and that sound came out; that great, great sound, that music.

" 'Fugue for Fleur,' " Ahmad whispered. Which was totally unnecessary, at least after that first bar. Kathy remembered what Fats had said about Fleur's voice making triads that you could see. That was what Harry was doing now. The music was distinctly Oriental. It tinkled. It fluttered like butterflies—artificial butterflies beating wings of fine spun gold. It bowed, pirouetted: two courtesans at the emperor's court, waving fans of jade. Bamboo fronds caught the breeze and moved, then froze again into a silken screen, hanging in a pagoda.

It was pure magic, and—Kathy realized with awe—pure genius, because anybody who could compose music like this had to be a genius. She sat there unmoving, listening to it. But, even so, she wasn't aware of exactly when it was that that note of heartbreak got into it. Because, before that, the electrician who controlled the lighting put a spotlight on Harry, and she saw the tears on his black face.

Quite suddenly, she couldn't breathe. It was, somehow, unspeakably awful that he should cry. And then his crying got into the music; the clarinet sobbed in triads like a whipped Oriental child. It was Death who pirouetted now, made the ceremonial gestures with the fans. The music soared, liquid silver, moonlight on a bamboo forest, cranes standing on one leg, listening, listening for—that last, that final visitor.

Who came. And then it ended. Abruptly. On a cry that combined the crash of a temple gong with a scream of stark-naked anguish. A sound you couldn't listen to. You simply couldn't. Only you had to.

"Kathy, please!" Ahmad said, his voice deep and troubled, and Kathy realized at long, long last that she was crying, too. She put up her bandaged hand to her face and her mascara blackened it. The very good, subdued, expensive makeup she used, so good you almost couldn't see it, was running down her face like the kind of junk you bought in the Prix Unique.

And then the silence hit her. Nobody had clapped. Nobody had even moved. They sat there like worshippers in a cathedral, almost prayerfully.

Until, as always, someone broke the spell. A girl. A member of Harry's cheering section, doubtless. She had all the characteristics: long lank hair, glasses on her nose, sandals on her bony feet. She screamed out in ecstasy, "'Arreee!" and before anyone could stop her she was up on the bandstand and had both arms wrapped around Harry's neck.

Then she was kissing him in a way that looked as if she were trying to inhale and swallow him at the same time. It went on and on, unbelievably. And—Kathy realized suddenly with a sense of shock that was a kind of very real and physical pain—unbearably.

"*Il ne faut pas donner ça*"—Ahmad's voice underlined the word '*ça*'—"more importance than it has. And it has none at all . . ."

Then Kathy saw that Fats was gently and humorously unwrapping the hysterical girl from around Harry; and then at last, out of relief probably, all the people in Le Blue Note clapped and cheered.

In the next half hour, Kathy Nichols drank three-quarters of a magnum of champagne.

When, finally, Harry came to her table and dropped wearily into a chair, Ahmad stood up.

"I will leave you, my children," he said. "Three—how is it that you say in English—is a confusion, no?"

"Don't go, Ahmad!" Kathy said sharply. "I—"

"You were enjoying my company," Ahmad said, "which has now become unnecessary. Besides, believe me Kathy, there are some things which cannot be postponed . . ."

"Stay and entertain her," Harry said slowly. "I'm tired. I'm afraid my conversation will be something less than bright . . ."

"Don't talk to her, then," Ahmad said. "Just hold her hand. Her left hand—the one she does not squeeze champagne glasses with. In any case, I have only one suggestion to make. Tomorrow being Sunday, why don't the two of you spend the day with me—*en famille*, of course—at my country place? I should be happy to send the car if—"

Harry looked at Kathy.

"I'd be delighted," she said.

"*D'accord*, then. I shall send the car early—at nine o'clock, say, since it is far to my place. Your apartment, Harry?"

"Yes, send it to my pad," Harry said.

"I will do that. Good-bye, my children. Be wise!"

Kathy sat there, wondering if there weren't something hidden in that phrase, too. In French, you always said to a child, "*Soyez sage*," instead of "*Soyez bon*." To be *sage* meant to pull your neck in, to be prudent, to hold your tongue in the presence of your elders. But the way Ahmad had said it—then she saw that Harry was looking at her and grinning a little.

"The girls' room is over there," he said, and pointed. "Go fix your face, Kathy. You're a mess."

"Oh!" Kathy said. "Harry, sometimes I *hate* you!"

"No, you don't," Harry said. "Go on, Kathy. Put your war paint back on. Make peepee while you're at it. You can't keep all that champagne on your insides. By now your tonsils must be floating—"

They were, Kathy realized suddenly.

"Oh, damn you, Harry!" she wailed, and fled.

When she came back again, she looked convincingly human. In fact, she would have looked positively angelic, if it hadn't been for a certain glint in her blue-green eyes.

She was, Harry saw, disposed to do battle; but for the life of him he couldn't figure over—or for—what. Which made it unanimous, because Kathy couldn't either.

"Harry," she said, "that girl—"

"What girl?" Harry said. "Lord, but you're pretty, Miss Anne!"

"Don't change the subject!" Kathy said. "That one—the one who was inhaling you, or devouring you, or both, up there on the bandstand—is she?"

"Is she what?" Harry said. He was grinning at her openly now, which wasn't helping her temper at all.

"Your little friend. I mean—in the French sense. *Ta petite amie*—hell, *ta 'tite maîtresse!*"

"Lord, Kathy, how would I know? Have to look in my stud book to see the last time I got bred. Not that that would help much—" His grin broadened. "All white women look just alike to me—"

She glared at him. But when she spoke her voice was strangely sweet.

"Harry, tell the waiter to set the table—"

"All right," Harry said. "Hungry, honeychile?"

"No. I need a knife. To cut your throat with," Kathy said.

Harry threw back his head and laughed aloud.

"I don't see what's so funny," Kathy said.

"You. Us. The world," Harry said. "But 'specially you. Yesterday you solemnly swore you'd shoot me if I tried to kiss you. Tonight you want to slice my neck because a little music lover confused music and musician —or wanted to be nice to this poor, downtrodden child of sin'n sorrow. Or something. Now you tell me, Miss Anne, is this a new kind of a put on? Or are you for real?"

Kathy considered that with the kind of seriousness that is often conveyed by three-quarters of a magnum of champagne. Then she proceeded to add another cup to her store.

"You're mine," she announced solemnly. "At least, that's what people are going to think. So for the—the duration—I make the rules. You've been—tormenting me—every way you could think up. And even if—no, not if!—though. And even *though* I have no intention of making use of your services—your extra—extra—extraordinary services—Ahmad said that—"

"Ahmad said *what?*" Harry said.

She grinned at him, her face the picture of mischief, half gamine and half sprite. Downed another cup of champagne.

" '*Comme homme, il est quelque chose de serieux, votre* 'Arree,' " she mimicked. "He said that. That's what the man said. Are you?"

"Am I what?" Harry said.

"*Quelquechose de serieux.* Are you, 'Arree?"

"You're drunk," Harry said.

"Right. Right as rain. But you haven't answered my question. Are you something serious in the hay?"

"The unanswerable question. Say 'It is a sign that a man's reputation is small and sinking when his own tongue must sing his praises,' *Bartlett's Familiar Quotations.* Or ask one of my cheering section. One of those faceless little girls whose deodorants don't work when they get excited. One of the little kittens who really are all gray in the dark . . . Or—"

"Or what?" Kathy said.

"Or would you rather have a demonstration? One

night when you're cold sober and mean it—but that *would* be something serious, I'm afraid."

"No," Kathy said. "No demonstrations. No free samples. No nothing. All the same, I don't mean . . . buy me some more champagne, Harry. This is all gone . . ."

"No," Harry said. "You've had enough."

"Then I'll buy you some. Only you'll have to pay for it. *Garçon! Encore un magnum de champagne, s'il vous plaît!*"

"*Quelle marque*, Mademoiselle?" the waiter said.

"Let me see. Let me see. Veuve Clicquot, *quarante-cinq*. Yes, Widow Klee Kote. Like me. I'm a widow. Or I'm going to be. A *grass* widow. Right, 'Arree?"

"*Pardon*, Mademoiselle?" the waiter said.

"It is nothing," Harry said. "Mademoiselle is amusing herself. Go bring her the champagne . . ."

"Yes, Mademoiselle *s'amuse!*" Kathy said. "And also she is drunk. *Ivre. Sous.* Verrreee drunk. Like an owl. Wanna hear me hoot?"

"Kathy, for God's sake," Harry said.

"All right. I'll be good, 'Arree. What were we talking about? *Quelquechose de serieux, n'est-ce pas?*"

"You were laying down the law to me," Harry said.

"Right. I remember. No demonstrations. But—all the same, my darlin' Harry, I don't mean to put you out to pasture, either. Want—my position—such as it is, such as it is—respected. Even if the whole thing is a put on to save me from—"

"The consequences of not keeping your miniskirt down and your minipanties up," Harry said solemnly.

"Of not keeping on a blessed stitch!" Kathy giggled. "Even if the whole thing—is—a put—a put on to save me from the results of having been a damn fool, it gives you no right to—hu—humiliate me, Harry. So kissing—other girls—is out. You don't kiss them. You don't kiss me. You don't kiss anybody. Clear?"

"Clear," Harry said. "What's not clear is why."

Kathy ignored that.

" 'Nother thing. You don't play—her music, anymore. You don't—stand up there with the tears running down your cheeks—and—and push me—clear off—off the world. Anni—anni—annihilate my existence. Know I—don't—don't matter to you. So you don't have to prove it—front of everybody—"

Harry stared at her.

"Do you *want* to matter to me, Kathy?" he said.

She stared back at him, owlishly.

"No. What I want is—is not to *not* matter."

"There's a difference?" Harry said.

"Yes. But don't make me explain it, now. I can't. Harry—"

"Yes, Kathy?"

"I don't want any more champagne. Take me home, won't you?"

"All right," Harry said.

The rest of it was rarely awful. While they waited for a cab, Kathy was singing:

"Dans la nuit, tous les chats sont gris
Sauf que 'Arree, car il est noir!
Gros chat noir dit meeow, meeow;
Gros chat noir dités moi, meeowww!"

"Meeow!" Harry said, and pushed her into the taxi.

Two minutes later, she said, "Harry, I'm gonna be sick!" And was. All over everything.

The taxi driver jammed on his brakes. Got out. Came around back. Looked in.

"You will remove your slut!" he screamed. "I knew it! The species of a whore who couches herself with *sales nègres* was sure to—"

Harry got out of the cab then. The cabby had stopped under a streetlamp so he could see Harry's face.

"*Au secours!*" he yelped. "*Police! Ce gros singe noir—*"

Then Harry hit him, very fast and very hard. Twice. Left him lying in the street, and dragged Kathy out of the taxi. Got his clarinet and case out, too. Left there, limping, half carrying Kathy. Three streets away, he found another cab.

When he finally got her to his flat, she was fast asleep. So he searched in her bag until he found the keys he'd given her. Then he opened the front door, and, after having carefully deposited his clarinet in the darkest part of the hall, carried Kathy up three flights of stairs in his arms as though she were a child. He opened the door to his flat with the second key. Clicked on the light with his elbow.

But when he put her down on the bed, she suddenly put both her arms around his neck. Without opening her eyes, she said,

"Harry—"

"Yes, Kathy?" he said.

"Don't go. Stay here with me and—"

"And what?" Harry said.

"Oh, you know!" she giggled, senselessly.

He put up his hands and broke her grip. Pushed her arms down to her sides. Stood there looking at her. Suddenly, gently, he bent and kissed her warm, slack, defenseless mouth. Her breath stank. Of vomit. Of champagne.

"Sleep tight, baby girl," he said.

Going down the stairs, the sadness he felt was a new kind, and very bad.

Chapter Four

When Harry knocked on that same door the next morning, it was a little after nine, and Kathy was still sleeping the sleep of the innocent, the good, the pure at heart.

"Get up," Harry said. "Ahmad's chauffeur's here with the car. And he's double-parked . . ."

"Oh, God!" Kathy said.

"Kathy—" Harry said.

"Tell him to circle the block. I have to shower at least, Harry! I have to! And—"

"No and's. You can put your war paint on in the car. It's a two-hour drive. That's time enough for even you to put on a new face—"

"All right—" Kathy said faintly. The words percolated through a yawn.

"C'mon, wench!" Harry roared. "Let me hear your feet hit that floor!"

"Oh, damn you, Harry!" Kathy said. But then she was up and scurrying about. Harry went back down the stairs.

"*Circulez*," he said to the chauffeur. "*Les femmes—*"

"You have no need to tell me," the chauffeur groaned. "I am married. I will return in half an hour. *D'accord*, M'sieu le Musicien?"

"No. Make it a quarter. She is not slow, this little one. Besides, here comes a *flic*."

The chauffeur turned the key and slammed down on the accelerator. Harry moved off down the street towards Emil's café. A coffee would help, he thought.

When Harry got back to his place, Kathy was standing on the *trottoir*. She looked very small, and lost, and forlorn. There were blue semicircles beneath her eyes. Without lipstick, her mouth was almost colorless. In sober fact, she looked exactly the way all pale blondes do early in the morning: awful. Harry found himself wondering if the cosmetics industry would ever have reached its present pinnacle if it hadn't been for the social ascendancy of the Nordic type. Brunettes, especially the Mediterranean breed, looked damned fine in the morning—even after a night of love. Better than ever, some of them, glistening with healthy sweat, glowing. But Kathy, without makeup, was like a snapshot in black and white compared to one in color. Her features, her exquisite bone structure, were as lovely as ever; but, the artificial alchemy of female witchcraft denied her, she looked sick. Leaning close, Harry saw that she actually was.

Her eyes, looking at him, were so dilated that only a thin rim of greenish-blue showed around the lightless black of their pupils. Their whites were red-streaked. Her lashes, without mascara, were dusty-straw. But the worst of it was the indefinable something that moved behind her eyes. He couldn't determine what that something was. But it wasn't pretty. It wasn't pretty at all.

"Harry—" she got out.

"Yes, Kathy?" he said.

"Did—did you?"

"Did I what?" Harry said.

She stared at him, but the words wouldn't come.

"You know—" she said.

"I *don't* know," Harry said. "Speak your piece, Miss Anne!"

"Don't call me 'Miss Anne' damnit! Did you—did you —make love to me—last night?"

Harry looked at her. A long time. A long slow dead stopped awful time.

"Don't you *know*?" he said.

She shook her bright head, miserably.

"No. There—there weren't any—any signs. But then, you—you might have used—a—a thing, so—"

"So?" Harry said.

"So, tell me! Did you make love to—"

"Wrong preposition. Not *to*—with. Did I make love with an inert female carcass, dead stinking drunk and smelling of puke? Is that what you want to know, Kathy?"

She stared at him, and her eyes went tear-blind.

"Oh, Harry!" she whispered. "I'm so ashamed!"

"Interesting development," Harry said. "What are you ashamed of now, Miss Anne?"

"Harry—I—I—propositioned you, didn't I? I just know I did! And you—"

"I said, 'Sleep tight, baby girl.' Not my cup of tea. I'd as soon lay a store-window dummy. Just as motionless, and probably warmer. Besides, I don't believe in that phrase 'in vino veritas.' Not at all . . ."

"Harry—" Her voice was the silence underneath sound. Looking at her hurt. It hurt physically. There is nothing uglier to watch than self-flagellation.

"Yes, Kathy?"

"Why didn't you?" she said bitterly. "I—I *wanted* you to!"

"Me?" Harry said. "Or the flic on the beat? Or the iceman, or the *facteur*, or anything in pants that happened by?"

"Right," Kathy said. "Anybody. When I get drunk— anybody will do. Anybody at all. That's why I never drink. Only I never thought I'd sink so low that—"

She stopped. Her chin started to shake. Her mouth. Her lips made a whitish blur. Her eyes were big with horror. The shame in them was stark-naked.

"Harry—" she said, "why don't you—hit me?"

"For not being a hypocrite?" Harry said. "For being honest? For telling the truth?"

"No. For not being honest. For not telling the truth. For talking like a polly parrot, saying things I've *heard* all my life without ever letting them go through my head. Or my heart, either—"

"Or maybe," Harry said wearily, "letting them go through too fast."

"Yes," she whispered. "You're right. Never hanging on to them long enough to—to look at them. To examine whether they make sense or not. That was—my mother talking then, Harry, not me. She would have said that. She—"

"Would *not*. The idea wouldn't have crossed the back part of her old-time Southern, lily-white mind. If you're starting in to be honest, don't muck the deal, Kathy. Being honest with yourself can be a bad trip. Worse than LSD. But if you make it back—"

"Back from where, Harry?"

"Hell. The real thing. Not something a wop poet dreamed up. A great wop poet and a great Hell. But not the real thing."

"What is the real thing?"

"Knowing yourself. Right down to the pimples on your behind. Funny thing, never met a blonde yet who didn't have 'em—"

"Didn't have *what*?" Kathy said.

"Pimples on her behind. Racial trait. Proof of superiority. Right, Josephine?"

"Josephine! And—and pimples! Harry, for Christ's sake! Why—"

"Josephine Reb. Can't call you Johnny, can I?"

"Oh, hell," she wept. "Oh, Christ. Oh, God. Oh, Jesus. I start in to say something and you twist it into knots. Knots that hurt! Harry, what *were* we talking about?"

"The moment of truth," Harry said solemnly.

She looked at him.

"You said that if—that if I made it back from the bad trip of being honest with myself—"

"Nothing could hurt you anymore, baby girl. You'll have got there. Seceded from the South. Joined the human race. And the next guy in your life will be there for the right reasons. 'Cause you love him. Because he makes you feel good all over, inside and out. And his camouflage job or the way his eyes slant won't matter a damn. Tell you another thing, Miss Anne—"

"What thing, Harry?"

"I prefer you—a good, tough, simpleminded bigot, to your opposite: the lily-white masochist, aching to make up for every shitty deal the whole white race ever pulled on us, or the curiosity-stricken dame who's been told that, as studs, we're the greatest, heavier hung and all that jazz, donchaknow. Don't want to be accepted or rejected because I'm black. But, of the two, I prefer being rejected. Easier to deal with. So now, do we *really* start being honest?"

"Yes. Harry, I—I told you I never drink because—"

"It gives you hot pants," Harry said.

"All right! I was going to say it makes me amorous, but let it go. I never drink, but last night I did. You know why, Harry?"

"No," Harry said.

"It was because you—you played *her* music. Played it and—"

"Pushed you off the world?"

"Yes. Harry—am I—am I—falling in love with you? In spite of your being black, I mean?"

Harry went on looking at her, said "Jesus H. Christ!" very softly.

"When—that girl kissed you, I didn't like it. I didn't like it at all. In fact, it made me madder'n old hell. But before that—you—you'd already convinced me that even dead—your—Fleur—was everything, and I was nothing— or even less—with that music. That strange, Chinesey music. So if there's a way to get to me, you've found it. I—I've always been—well, front and center, sort of. Most popular girl in the class. Miss Hill Crest, '65. Cotton Bowl Queen. 'The lovely Kathy Nichols who—' "

"Had to cop out. Take a powder. Get the hell out from under the spreading magnolia tree. So now, here she is in Gay Paree, the saddest goddamned burg in the world, the only place on God's green earth where she could fall into the clutches of—of a Mau Mau. A witch doctor. Making with the masks, the signs, the rattles. A voodoo artist, snowing her with *gris-gris*, bending her sweet simple mind—because she persists in the prejudices she was born to. Trying to play Pygmalion. Or that Bernard Shaw character who screwed poor Eliza Doolittle's life up for her. And also, My Fair Lady Kathy, because you are pretty and sweet and so damned innocent that even letting yourself get laid by creeps doesn't damage you. Tell me something, honeychile. You ever come?"

"Har—ry!"

"I beg your pardon, Miss Anne. Did you ever experience an orgasm?"

"Of course! Why, what do you think I—"

"I think you're lying again," Harry said. "And anyhow, here comes the car."

Before they were out of Paris, Harry looked down at her hand. The bandage was a sodden mess, and dirty to boot. So he made Muhammad stop the car in front of a pharmacy, and bought clean gauze, sulfamide powder, and adhesive tape. Then he proceeded to strip off the old bandage, dust the cut with powder, and rebandage her hand. When he'd finished that, she looked at him wonderingly.

"Harry—are you good? Or are you—evil, sort of? I can't figure out which."

"Don't try, Miss Anne," Harry said. "Here, put your little head on my shoulder and go to sleep. That way, you can quit thinking. Lousy business, thinking—"

Obediently, she rested her head against his shoulder, closed her eyes.

"Hmmmmmm," she murmured, "you smell so nice!"

"Compulsive behavior, honeychile," he said sadly. "We're supposed to stink, so a long time ago I got into the habit of bathing twice a day. Changing from the skin out. Rubbing every variety of funk-killer known to man into my black hide. Because an American Negro isn't a man—he's a walking defense mechanism—"

She straightened up suddenly; looked at him.

"Now *you're* being honest, too!" she said.

"I usually am," Harry said.

"Yes—but honest-sarcastic, not honest-honest like now. I like you much better this way."

She put her head back down on his shoulder.

"Harry—" she said.

"Yes, baby girl?"

"I—I *was* lying. I never have."

"You never have *what*?"

"Oh, you know! What we were talking about. I—I like making love, but I never seem to get much out of it."

"Meaning you don't know how to pick your studs," Harry said.

She giggled, suddenly.

"Is this a snow job, Harry?" she said.

"You ever see a charcoal snowman?" Harry said.

"Yes," Kathy said, "*you*."

"Oh, hell, Kathy, go to sleep. You're getting *me* confused, and I don't like it."

"Good!" she said. "I like confusing you. Harry, where are we going?"

"To Ahmad's house."

"I know that, damnit! But where is Ahmad's house?"

"In the country—about forty kilometers south of Saint-Cloud. You go out the Porte d'Italie and take Nationale Sept, as though you were going to Cannes or Nice. Once past Saint-Cloud, you turn off on a cloverleaf intersection that's so complicated I always get lost on it. But Muhammad can do it every time. Is it not so, Muhammad?"

"*Quoi*, M'sieu Harry?" Muhammad said. Like all those whose mother tongue is Arabic, Muhammad had no trouble pronouncing the aspirate 'H.'

"Nothing," Harry said. "I make small talk. It is necessary to keep them amused, the little girls . . ."

"Harry," Kathy said. "Turn me loose. I have to put my makeup on. If Ahmad sees what I *really* look like, he'll think you're crazy . . ."

"I am," Harry said. "But anyhow, *allez-y*, Miss Anne!"

Ahmad's house was beautiful. It had a thatched roof —although it turned out later that the rushes were imitation, made of non-flammable plastic—and dormer windows in the upper story. The ground-floor windows and the glass doors of the ground floor were huge. The lawn was perfect, and the garden a marvel. It was grand style, which meant that every shrub, every tree, every bush had been clipped into sculptured designs à la Versailles. The idea that nature was beautiful in itself and should damned well be let alone had found small acceptance among the French, Harry reflected. Ahmad's formal garden was truly beautiful; but it was also, curiously, at one and the same time, monstrous. Like the French, themselves, he thought. Then, conceding at once that his thought was at least mildly, if not grossly unfair, he amended it to 'like the human race . . .'

Muhammad stopped the car, hopped out, opened the door for them. Harry took Kathy by the arm.

"How lovely!" she said.

"It is, isn't it?" he said. "Now, come on . . ."

They started up the flagstone walk towards the house; but, before they got there, two Sudanese houseboys dressed in elaborately embroidered burnooses, and wearing red fezzes on their heads, came flapping out to greet them, their white teeth flashing in their black faces.

"M'sieu Harry!" they chorused. "Welcome to Les Granges. And you, also, Madame!"

Harry shook hands with them, which, since they were servants, he shouldn't have. And which was why, maybe, he did it. Or maybe it was because they were black. He didn't know. And he didn't want to think about it, because considering what it meant to be black anywhere on the face of the globe, including Africa itself, was a bad trip, the worst, so he avoided it in the same way most people avoid thinking about their own deaths. That's what being black is, he thought, a species of death by inches, daily. When it isn't something worse: the annihilation of personality, the . . .

But seeing his gesture, Kathy, too, put out her slim, freckled hand to the two Negroes. To her vast astonishment, instead of shaking hands with her, both of them kissed her hand, almost reverently.

"M'sieu Ahmad and his family are at the tennis courts," one of them said to Harry. "You and your lady are to join them, there. He also instructed us to supply you with racquets and tennis clothes if you care to play . . ."

"I care to, but I cannot," Harry said simply. "A little accident to my leg makes running about for me an impossibility. But if *votre patron* would care to lend me a riding habit and that frisky gray of his, I should be happy to jump a few hedges—"

Then he saw Kathy staring at him.

"You—you ride?" she said.

"Sure, Miss Anne. Learned on an old broken-down mule, down on the farm. Then one time I stole the bossman Cap'n Rightoff's hoss, and—"

"Har—ry—" Kathy said.

"All right," he grinned at her. "One of the things that flossy boys' school Mom sent me to in Switzerland provided was riding lessons. Of course, I did most of my practice at night on *les filles* I sneaked out of Le Rosarie, but—"

"Harry, you're terrible. But if you're going to ride, so will I—if they've a horse to lend me, that is. I play awful tennis—"

"Is it possible, Feisal?" Harry said.

"But of course, M'sieu Harry! The little bay of Madame is sufficiently docile for Mademoiselle. Will you please lift your jacket, sir?"

Harry lifted his sport jacket waist-high.

"*Non,*" the houseboy said. "There is not the difficulty. The riding *pantalons* of M'sieu Ahmad will fit you . . ."

"Harry," Kathy whispered, "they aren't going to ask me to lift my skirt, are they?"

"Why should they?" Harry grinned at her. "It's practically a belt, now. Good thing you've got nice legs, baby. And Mademoiselle?" he said to the Sudanese.

"Even less. She is like a gazelle, so the riding dress of Mademoiselle Ouija will fit her perfectly. Even the boots, I think. Now, M'sieu, Dame, follow us. M'sieu Ahmad has reserved a chamber where you may change. We will bring you the riding habits at once—"

"A chamber!" Kathy whispered. "Harry, for God's sake! I—"

"Shhhh!" Harry said. "We'll manage."

It wasn't too difficult. Harry sat in the big high-backed *fauteuil* while she changed. It wasn't until after he'd turned it away from her that he noticed that by slanting his gaze to the left, he could see her reflection in the full-length mirror. Gallantry struggled briefly with curiosity. Being entirely male, as he was, curiosity won. In her minipanties and bra, she was glorious. At once Harry's nightshade sense of humor got the better of him.

"You do, you know," he said solemnly.

"I do *what*?" Kathy said.

"Have pimples on your behind," Harry said.

"Why!" Kathy said. "What a perfectly filthy trick! I could kill you, Harry! I could! I really could!"

Then she put out both her hands and dragged the mirror around so that he couldn't see her anymore.

"All right," she said at last; "I'm ready. You can change now."

"Okay," Harry said. "Get out of here. Go wait in the hall, Miss Anne."

She grinned at him then, her freckled face alight with mischief.

"No, I won't," she said. "I'm going to get even with you for peeking!"

She sat down on a fragile Louis Quinze chair, facing him. "All right, Harry," she mocked, "start your striptease!"

He grinned back at her.

"No sweat, Miss Anne! Never was modest. 'Sides, all the chicks tell me I'm mighty fine . . ."

He stood up, stripped off his jacket, tie, shirt.

"Harry—" Kathy said.

"Yes, Miss Anne?"

"They're right. The girls who told you that. You really are built. That's truly turning the other cheek, isn't it? After what you said about my poor little *derrière*, I mean. But it's true. You must have been a great athlete . . ."

"Evolution," Harry said, "or the lack of it. Mankind sprang from the ape, according to Darwin. Only we didn't spring far enough, Miss Anne. Smaller cranium, longer arms, shorter waist, stronger Achilles tendon, skinnier ass—"

"Utter rot," Kathy said. "Go on, let's see whether you have pretty legs!"

"Now you've got me blushing," Harry said. "Trouble is, with my rosy-pink complexion, you can't see it. Used to call me the Head Kleagle of the lily whites, down home. Now get out of here, Kathy! Scat!"

" 'S not fair," Kathy teased. "You looked at my poor little pimply bottom, and now you won't let me see your pretty legs!" But she went, all the same.

The minute she was gone, Harry took off his pants. Then he bent and began to massage the back of his right leg. It had stiffened up on him in the car. And if he were going to ride, he had to loosen it up a little. Besides, it hurt like hell. But it took him some time to get it back to a state approaching normal. So long, in fact, that Kathy suddenly pushed open the door, and stuck her bright, tousled head in.

"Aren't you ready, yet?" she began—"oops! I'm sorry!" Then, "How—how awful!" she breathed.

He turned, clad only in his boxer shorts, still, and saw how she was staring at that hideous scar, at the wasted calf of his right leg.

"Dog bit me," he said solemnly. "Little Pekinese no bigger than—" Then he saw she was very close to tears. "Don't, Kathy—" he said.

"I thought we'd quit lying to each other," she whispered. "That's another souvenir of Vietnam, isn't it?"

Harry picked up Ahmad's riding pants, stepped into them, zippered up the fly. Put out his hand for the pearl-gray turtleneck sweater lying on the bed.

"That was my ticket home," he said. "Only I couldn't stay when I got there. Mr. Charley wouldn't let me. Not with Fleur, that is. Brought her home to visit Mom and the old man on the basis of rumors I'd heard that the States were getting civilized. Should have known better. Coppers grabbed us before we even got to the house. Had a roadblock waiting half a mile from the airport. Radio. Come to think of it, that *is* civilized, isn't it? Radio and electric cattle prods and high-pressure hoses and tear gas and dynamite in churches blowing the heads off of baby girls . . ."

"Oh, please!" Kathy said.

"Georgia law: 'No gawddamn burrheaded liverlipped son of his mother can crawl into the hay with thuh purity of Southern white womanhood 'n that's a nach'l fact! Not even if he's married to her—' "

"But—but," Kathy said, "your Fleur wasn't—"

"White. Exactly, Miss Anne! You're really in there, right on the beam, as usual, aren't you? Not that any law that says whom I can or can't marry isn't the ultimate violation of human liberty, but that I hadn't really broken said law 'cause Fleur was sort of tan herself. Right. Right as rain! Funny thing—that was precisely the defense my lawyer-man used to spring me. That Orientals are *untermenschen,* too. That the *Herrenvolk* shouldn't pay no 'tention nohows if a cullud boy gits hisself a lil' yellow nookie crosswise Chinee style. Got me off—on condition that we leave town within twenty-four hours. Coppers escorted us to the airport. So we went to New York—"

"And?" Kathy whispered.

"Found more of the same. Subtler, but the same shitty

deal. Marriage is *not* a private matter when your hides don't match. Tell you one thing, Kathy—there isn't anywhere in the U.S.A., from Augusta, Maine, to Miami, Florida, from Montauk Light to 'Frisco Bay, a black boy can live. Nowhere at all . . ."

"That's why you said you lived nineteen million years in Georgia. Harry! That's another one I caught you on! You said your folks sent you to Switzerland when you were thirteen years old. So how—"

"Could I have spent nineteen million years in Georgia? Easy. I'm an only child. Mom carted me back across the Atlantic every summer. Made it worse—contrasting Switzerland and Georgia, I mean . . ."

"Your family must have had an awful lot of money," Kathy said.

"They did," Harry said. "One of the by-products of segregation. Makes the smart Negroes rich. Black folks couldn't get into the local hospital even if they were dying. One of the greatest blues singers of all time died of that. Bled to death after a car smashup because there was no place to take her. So the old man built a private clinic. And he was *good.* Half the poor whites in the county used to come to him, after dark. When the black bourgeoisie found out he wasn't making the undertaker rich, that he could snatch a kid, an appendix, or a pair of tonsils, and the patient mostly walked away from surgery a few weeks later, they swore by him. So he graduated from a Model-A Ford to a black Caddy so long he had to hinge it in the middle to turn the corner. The mayor put him on the City Advisory Board, race-relations, that is—and—" He stopped suddenly and a grin crinkled the corners of his eyes. By that time he'd finally succeeded in easing the second of the pair of riding boots over the calf of his bad leg.

"Kathy, baby, you know what Ahmad *et famille* are going to think we're doing up here if we don't quit talking and get down to the courts?" he said.

"Good Lord!" Kathy said. "Come on!"

Chapter
Five

"Harry," Ahmad said gaily, "it is far better for the health to take your exercise in the open air—"

"Not to mention the morals, eh, M'sieu Zahibuine?" Kathy said mischievously.

"The morals?" Ahmad said. "But what, my so very beautiful little Kathy, are they?"

"Something *you* know nothing of, my husband," a woman's voice said; and Harry stood there, watching what Kathy's eyes and mouth did when she saw Madame Zahibuine for the first time. Ahmad's wife was little and plump, and very pretty. She was also clearly of mixed Arabic and Negro ancestry, for her skin was very dark, a burnt-chocolate color. She wore her Negroid kinky hair *au naturel*, which is to say that neither hot irons nor pomades had ever touched it, for it covered her head in the rounded, woolly, ball-shaped coiffure that black coeds in the States were already beginning to affect as a symbol of their liberation from the whiteman's standards of beauty. She got up from the chaise lounge she'd been lying on beside the nearest of the three tennis courts, and came towards them.

"So," she purred in her beautifully articulated, almost too musical French, "this is the little Kathy who has taught our Harry to smile again! We are very grateful to you for that, my dear—"

Shyly Kathy put out her hand to her. But, instead of shaking it, Madame Zahibuine drew Kathy gently towards her.

"I should like to kiss you, if you don't mind, *ma chérie*," she said. "Since you are going to marry Harry, we are going to be friends, is it not so? Harry is like a son to us—"

"A very big son for so small a mother," Kathy said, and kissed her cheek. "How do you call yourself, Madame Zahibuine?"

"Dhahaba," Madame Zahibuine said. "Now you will come and meet the children . . ."

"Ah, yes," Ahmad said. "They are strangely silent. And when they are silent, I worry. The mischief they are getting into is likely to be serious in such a case—"

"He is worried about our daughter, Ouija, who is a

teenager," Dhahaba said to Kathy. "My Ahmad pretends to be very modern, but at heart he is a Moorish sultan. Come . . ."

The children—a fair-sized army of them—had all the tennis courts occupied, and were wrestling and playing rugby on the lawn. A huge man, so broad and muscular that he made his own six feet-one look short, stood by a tree, watching them very carefully. Harry saw Kathy's eyebrows rise at that. He bent close to her ear.

"Ahmad's gorilla," he whispered. "Bodyguard, to you. Needs one. El Fatah tried to snatch little Hagib a while back. If it *was* El Fatah. Don't know what Ahmad's home-country politics were. Heard he supported Ben Bella. Figures. He's never been back, not even on a visit. But most likely it was El Fatah—trying to put the squeeze on him for more contributions to the cause . . ."

He went on watching her face as she stared at that horde of children. It was easy to distinguish the Zahibuine children from the others—invited friends, surely—because they looked like either one or the other of their parents, and sometimes like both. But one thing about Ahmad's offspring was indisputable: From seventeen-year-old Ouija—who, for the moment, and to Harry's acute disappointment, was nowhere to be seen—down to the youngest, a toddler still falling over his fat little feet, they were very beautiful children indeed.

Harry stood there watching Kathy's face as she digested that fact, and beyond that, its implications, which added up to at least the possibility that everything she'd thought, believed, accepted, been taught all her life was dead, damned wrong.

"Ethically, scientifically, and de facto," he said.

"Harry, what on earth—" Kathy began.

"Those kids," he said. "They shouldn't be gorgeous, but they are. Ever visit a ranch, Miss Anne?"

"Yes," Kathy said. "My Uncle Tony has one. In California. Horses and cattle, mostly—"

"Then you shouldn't look so surprised. Crossing, done right, always improves the breed."

She looked at him then.

"Stop snowing me, Harry," she said.

"Wrong word. Say 'educating,' Miss Anne. Now forget it. We'd better—"

"No," Kathy said, "I won't forget it. Since what's between us is—only temporary—what are you educating me for, Harry? What good will it do you?"

"No good. But you, maybe, some. Besides, there's one other possibility—"

"What possibility?"

"That from now on, in spite of yourself, baby girl, you're going to be my guided missile. Soon as I get you aimed right, that is—"

"Har—ry! That one you'd better explain. It sounds—"

"Lord awful. Could be. Depends on your point of view. Now let's drop it, honeychile. It would take hours to get it through your weird little head, and right now we've got to be polite."

"*Mes enfants*," Dhahaba called out, "Look who has come to visit us!"

"Har—ree!" the children squealed and came swarming. The younger ones climbed all over Harry, kissing his cheeks and swinging around his neck. But the older ones were more reserved. A boy of fifteen or so and the exact duplicate of Ahmad except for a shoulder-length mop that would have branded him an effeminate as little as ten years before, but which was now an accepted part of the scheme of things, came forward and put out his hand to Harry.

"*Mes félicitations, mon cher*," he said gravely. "*Elle est vraiment quelquechose, ta petite blonde—*"

"Ahmad, Second," Harry said to Kathy, then turning back to the boy. "And where is Ouija? I very much want Kathy to meet her—"

"Over there," Ahmad Second said, and pointed in the direction of the swimming pool which, though it was far too cool for swimming that first week in May, was already being filled by one of the gardeners. "With Raoul Levi. He's our latest *héros*. Grace of *les flics*. They cracked his head for him the other day. At the Sorbonne. He objected too strenuously to being thrown into the salad basket with the rest of the types who came down from Nanterre with Cohn-Bendit—you have heard of him, is it not so? Danny the Red?—to start trouble. To hear Raoul tell it, it took a full squad of the CRS to do him in. Seems he fought most valiantly—"

"Waving the red flag in one hand and the thoughts of Mao Tse-tung in the other?" Harry asked.

"Exactly. *Un salaud*, but charming. Shall I call them?" young Ahmad said.

"Do," Dhahaba said. Then, turning to Harry, she added, "I do not like this boy. Not only is he a Jew, but his influence on Ouija is—too strong."

"You—you object to his being Jewish, Madame Zahibuine?" Kathy said.

"I, no," Dhahaba sighed. "But my husband has, I'm afraid, strong feelings on that subject—"

Kathy looked at Harry. She went on looking at him a

long time. In fact, she was still looking at him when she spoke, so it was with a kind of shock that he realized it was to Ahmad she was talking and not to him.

"M'sieu Zahibuine," she said sweetly, "don't you like Jewish people?"

Ahmad stretched out his legs, long and hairy below his tennis shorts and grinned at her.

"Does anybody?" he said.

"I do," Harry said solemnly.

"*Ah, non, mon cher!*" Ahmad said. "You admire them. Possibly you respect them. Almost surely you envy the way they control the world. For that matter, so do I. But you do not *like* them. That, my dear Harry, simply is not possible . . ."

Harry opened his mouth to say a short and expressive French word. But then he saw how two of Ahmad's children, a boy and a girl, about nine and ten years old, were staring at him, their darkly beautiful faces alight with mischievous expectation. So he compromised.

"*Le mot de* Cambronne," he said.

"Harry," Kathy said, "there you go again! Always talking riddles! What is the word of Cambronne?"

"*Merde*," the nine-year-old said happily. "Which in your language means 'shit,' Mademoiselle—"

"We are *very* advanced," Dhahaba laughed. "Now for that, you little villains, I forbid you to stay here any longer! March yourselves! *De suite!*"

"Ah, *Maman!*" the children protested, looking pleadingly at Harry all the time.

"Scat," Harry said. "Go drown yourselves. I intend to teach your Papa all the rest of the words in the good General's vocabulary. But first, Hagib, tell me, what do the history books say that General Cambronne said to the English when they had him surrounded and demanded that he render himself and his forces?"

" 'The old guard dies, but it never surrenders!' " the boy piped.

"And what did he really say?" Harry said.

" '*Merde!*' " little Hagib said happily.

"Good," Harry said. "Now that you've learned that history books aren't to be trusted, you have already proved yourself smarter than your Papa. He even believes in Radio Cairo. Go on—run over there behind the hedges and play kissing games with the little girls—"

"Like you and Mademoiselle upstairs?" Hagib said. "Taking three-quarters of an hour to change into riding clothes?"

"*Touché!*" Ahmad roared. "Be off with you, limb of Shaitan! And you, too, Fatima. But no kissing games, you hear me?"

"*Oui, Papa,*" Fatima said. "*Tiens!* If there were not so many of us, one would think you'd never learned there are more interesting ways of making love!"

With that, the two of them scampered off, while Harry rocked back and forth in silent laughter. But even so, even then, he was watching Kathy. Manning her ramparts, he thought wryly, bringing up her heavy artillery. Oh, brother, here she goes!

"M'sieu Ahmad," Kathy said, "why don't you like the Jews?"

"Several million reasons," Ahmad said, "which, being instinctive, have very little justification, I fear. But reasonably and justifiably because it seems to me that throughout history they have been troublemakers. For instance, one of them, Karl Marx, invented Communism. Another, Leon Trotsky, greatly extended it. And even today, their youngsters like this Cohn-Bendit, and even this particularly odious young *salaud* Ouija is too fond of, are in the forefront of the peculiar and dangerous student rebellion. But most of all because they have stolen lands that have always been ours, dispossessed hundreds of thousands of our people, created problems that—"

But, by then, finally, Ahmad Second was back with his sister Ouija and young Raoul Levi, *le héros* of the second student battle. The first one, delivered in full fury by handsome young Daniel Cohn-Bendit and his *enragés* over a whole spectrum of totally undigested ideas, the chief of which seemed to have been their objection to not being allowed by the university authorities to spend their nights in the bedrooms of their sweethearts in the girls' dormitory, had forced the closing of the University of Nanterre on March 22. The second one, caused by the summoning of Cohn-Bendit and his band before the Central University Authorities at the Sorbonne, had taken place only a few days ago, on May 3. And now Peyrefitte, the Minister of Education, had closed the Sorbonne, too.

But, Harry suspected, the malaise went deeper than the causes the students espoused: Maoism, Trotskyism, anarchy, free love, student control of the great centers of learning, the elimination of examinations. It was a new thing in the history of man, the rebellion of the soft, the pampered, the well-off, so cloistered and so ignorant that they believed that they could do what neither Christ nor Marx had been able to do: purify society, change the nature of man. So, like spoiled children with a toy that no longer pleased them, they were out to smash the world they didn't like, get rid of duty, responsibility—even thought—as irksome, replace them with—what? Even they, Harry thought, don't know . . .

But he wasn't looking at the three youngsters. He was watching Kathy. He wanted to see how she was going to cope with the reality of Ouija, what arrangements all her preconceived notions were going to have to make among themselves to accommodate the absolutely stunning physical beauty—which not only equalled her own, but effortlessly exceeded it—of this crossbred daughter of two presumably inferior races.

What Kathy did was to stop breathing. Quite noticeably for a long, long moment. Then, just before the three youngsters were close enough to hear her, she bent and whispered into Harry's ear.

"If you could guarantee me a daughter who'd look like *that*, so help me, I'd *let* you!"

Harry grinned at her.

"That, present circumstances being considered," he drawled, "would be quite a trick, Miss Anne!"

"Oh, damn you, Harry!" Kathy wailed. "Did you *have* to remind me?"

" 'Arree," Ouija said, *"Elle est très belle, ta 'tite fiancée.* Is she a movie star?"

"Why, thank you, child!" Kathy laughed—a little shakily, Harry thought—"but it is *you* they should star, if beauty means anything."

"I have often thought of it as a career," Ouija said gravely, "but Papa does not approve. He is *très démodé, mon père.* Well, do we shake hands, or do I kiss you?"

"You kiss me," Kathy said, "for you have made me very happy, indeed . . ."

Ouija kissed her, then said,

"Why have I made you happy, Mademoiselle? Surely not by merely lending you my riding habit?"

"Because—because—" Kathy floundered.

"Because she thinks our children might possibly look like you," Harry supplied, gently.

"And if they do not, what difference does it make?" Raoul Levi said.

"None," Kathy said, "but I'd rather that they did."

"Then," Raoul said, "you have the typical bourgeois prejudices."

Harry stared at him. *That*, he thought, is *my* bit, son. Don't you go spoiling it for me . . .

"I," he said, "have never met anyone who was free of prejudices, M'sieu Levi. Certainly I am not."

Raoul Levi flopped down beside him.

"Call me Raoul," he said. "In you, they are justifiable."

"That, no," Harry said. "Prejudices are justifiable in no one. The color of my skin gives me no more right to hate people than the shape of your nose gives you—"

"Ha!" Ahmad Second said. "I warned you, Raoul, that Harry was a true intellectual and *very* clever."

"I see that, *mon vieux*," Raoul said. "And it pleases me. Now I can escape being bored. All you rich, liberal bourgeois bore me. I should prefer your being reactionaries. Then we could have some very amusing battles—"

"I," Ahmad Senior said ominously, "am reactionary enough to suit you, *jeune homme*. I believe the business of students is to study, not to fight the police—"

"Ahmad!" Dhahaba said. "He is our guest!"

"Unhappily," Ahmad said. "I am an Arab, Monsieur Levi, and among us, a guest is sacred. Which is why I have not yet shot or drowned you. But do not try my patience too far—"

"Papa!" Ouija said.

"Do not fear, *ma petite*," Raoul said. "It is not necessary to consider the ideas of *ton père's* generation. They count for nothing. And besides—" he grinned at Ahmad Senior, mockingly, "he is only *one* Arab. Surely recent events should have demonstrated to him that that proportion is grossly insufficient . . ."

Ahmad was halfway out of his chair when Ouija flung herself upon him. She put her arms about his neck.

"Papa, please!" she said.

Kathy was staring at Raoul Levi.

"Is it the custom among the Jews," she said, her voice shaking a little from fury, "to be rude to those who have extended you their hospitality?"

Raoul grinned at her.

"Hardly," he said. "But then I follow neither the religion nor the customs of *les Juifs, ma belle,* since both have always resulted in our getting massacred."

"What you don't follow, *mon* Raoul," Ouija said from where she sat on her father's lap, "is simple courtesy. You are, I am afraid, very badly brought up."

"On the contrary," Raoul laughed, "I was extremely *bien élevé. Maman*—she invented correction, *tu sais. Et Papa!* In comparison to him, *ton père* is Che Guevara resurrected. Only I rejected my background. For what does it serve, the education of a society that is going to disappear? That it is our *duty* to destroy?"

Harry stared at him.

"And with what will you replace it, Raoul?" he said.

"One thing at a time, *mon vieux!*" Raoul said cheerfully. "First we destroy it. Then we improvise. For whatever we replace it with cannot possibly be worse than what you old ones have handed down to us . . ."

"Of all the insufferable—" Kathy began, but Harry cut her off.

"If," he said, "you had been studying your history, Raoul Levi, instead of exchanging *coups* with the flics, you would be less sure of that. The Roman Empire was destroyed about A.D. 475, to accept a quite arbitrary date. And up until well past the First World War, Europeans were not as well-fed, and certainly a great deal less well-washed than they were under the rule of Augustus Caesar—"

"How American!" Raoul quipped. "Tell me, *mon cher*, do you always confuse civilization with plumbing?"

"And you, *mon cher* representative of the younger generation, do you not confuse it with throwing paving stones at *les flics*? With free love? With the pompous idiocies of Mao Tse-tung? Tell me, *mon gars*, what is it really that you believe?"

"In Negritude, for one thing," Raoul said. "But you intrigue me, 'Arry. Turn about is fair play. First you tell me—what do *you* believe?"

Harry smiled.

"In *le bourgeoisie*, in the first place, since it is the source of all things, even revolutionaries. From what class did Danton, Robespierre, Marat, et al., come? Kerensky, Lenin, Stalin, Trotsky, and even Marx himself? Fidel Castro, Ernesto 'Che' Guevara, and your so dearly-beloved Mao Tse-tung? When have you ever heard of a *worker* starting a revolution?"

Raoul nodded gravely.

"Good," he said. "Continue, I pray."

"All right," Harry said. "In the second place, I believe that the chief virtues in a world where mindless rebellion has become too fashionable are a reasonable degree of conformity, some measure of adaptability to one's circumstances, however unpleasant, and the at least nominal fidelity of women, since, without these things, civilization simply is not possible—"

"*Tiens!*" Raoul Levi said. "You really *are un bourgeois!*"

"You honor me," Harry said. "I know of nothing finer to be. Certainly not a revolutionary, because no revolution has ever settled, or even improved, anything . . ."

"But you do believe in war, do you not?" Raoul said. "I am told you fought in Vietnam."

"You were told the truth. But I do not believe in war, either. All it does, at the cost of uncounted lives and untold misery, is to postpone the settlement at the conference table, what should have been settled there beforehand . . ."

"Then why did you fight—and in the Army of the oppressors of your own people at that!—to suppress the liberties of the free, democratic peoples of Vietnam?"

"*Merde,*" Harry said. "Which is what you should leave out of this, this total *merde* of revolutionary cant. I grant you that there is a fine excess of feces in our corrupt bourgeois society as well. But substituting one variety of *merde* for another doesn't help anything. You know what the Chinese ideograph for 'liberty' means, literally? Did not the little red book of the little red mind of little fat Mao Tse-tung, who additionally writes unforgivably bad poetry, tell you that?"

"Harry!" Kathy said, clapping her hands delightedly like a child. "What a phrase! Go on, give it to him!"

"Shut up, baby," Harry said. "Do you, Raoul?"

"No," Raoul said. "What does it mean, literally?"

" 'Organized confusion.' And I don't think the Vietnamese even have a word for it. How could we rob them of what they have never possessed? Of what they don't even value, preferring something they call 'face' to it?"

"Then," Raoul said, "what *were* you doing in Vietnam, 'Arry?"

"Proving something to myself," Harry said sadly. "That I still had balls. That the life of a black man in white America hadn't robbed me of them—"

"And yet you fought for your white oppressors," Raoul mocked.

"No. I fought for me. To find out who—or *what*—I am. More *merde*. I still don't know—"

"Harry," Kathy said in English, "being honest is all right, I guess, but being *that* honest is sick. Especially with this creep—"

"Have you then, no pride of race, *mon* 'Arree?" Ouija put in suddenly.

"No," Harry said. "None. Aside from the fact that, logically speaking, a biological accident is hardly sufficient motive for self-congratulation, the only race I believe in is the human race, and its record, throughout history, has been abysmal. But if it is of *les Noirs* that you speak, even less. I should have preferred to have been born a Comanche, an Iroquois, or a Sioux, who died before accepting slavery. What I truly believe, I suppose, is in the guilt of the victim. If your people, Raoul, had started fighting from the beginning, instead of waiting until Warsaw to make that last, totally admirable stand, there would have been no Auschwitz, Dachau, Mannerheim. Even if one cannot win, one can choose the manner of one's dying—"

"And that manner is?" young Levi said.

"That it be costly to *les assassins*," Harry said. "That, confronted with absolute evil, one should resist absolutely. That the death of one cornered cat is more admirable than that of a whole herd of sheep. As some of your people at least have learned. They proved it quite recently—"

"Go on, M'sieu le Philosophe!" Raoul Levi said.

"I believe," Harry went on quietly, "that every crime is to some extent a contract between victim and criminal. Accepted by the victim. For nothing, *mon gars*, can happen to a man that he won't *permit* to happen. By which I mean, if one is prepared to pay the price necessary to maintain one's integrity, one's dignity, one's humanity, one can never be robbed of them. At worst, all one can be robbed of is life, which, without these things is nothing, *en tout cas*. So while I do not absolve the lordly white race of its unspeakable inhumanity towards every other variety of mankind that differs from it even slightly—the Opium Wars and the Sepoy Mutiny come readily enough to mind—I find that the black man bears a burden of guilt only a little less heavy. For if my people had *ever* learned not to decimate one another in insanely ferocious tribal wars, if it had occurred to any of them that whatever one might do with an enemy captive of one's own race, it was *not* permissable, say, to sell him to a white slaver—"

"Harry," Kathy said, "I didn't know—"

"That fully seventy percent of the Negroes who became slaves in the Antilles, in North and South America, were sold into slavery by other Negroes? They were, my dear. And often for no more serious crime than petty thievery and falling into debt. Younger brothers sold older brothers to clear their way to the succession to some tribal kingship. Husbands sold troublesome wives. But the chief source, of course, were the members of another tribe captured in a tribal war, which soon enough, under the benign and civilizing influence of the oh-so-civilized white race, degenerated into manhunts, pure and simple. Ibo sold Hausa with great glee. And the Ashanti and Dahomean sold all the rest. Of course—" Harry grinned ruefully at Ahmad—"our Arab friends made up the slack by raiding—"

"Now, Harry—" Ahmad said, "that was a long time ago, and—"

"Agreed. *D'accord*," Harry said. "Besides, it is the guilt of the victim I am discussing, not that of the oppressor. It needs discussion, being less obvious. My people, *le bon Dieu* pity them! What have we? Whom can we boast of? The late Patrice Lumumba? Moïse Tshombe? Papa Doc Duvalier and his *Tontons Macoute*? The genocides of Nigeria who hired Egyptian pilots to blast the brains out of other black heads, and then loosed dogs innoculated with rabies upon the Biafran women and children hiding—and starving at the rate of one thousand per day—in brush? The soldiers of the Congolese Army who dined upon fricasseed nuns?

"The one blessed exception I can think of is Houphouët-Boigny, and even he runs the Ivory Coast by making use of white Frenchmen to manage every gov-

ernment office and every business where the slightest
degree of brains and skill is necessary, while—hopefully—
training black civil servants and technicians to take over
later. If my people had ever produced anything remotely
resembling a civilization—and spare me, *je vous en prie!*
that *merde* about Timbuktu, which was an imported
Islamic culture of which even the language was Arabic!
—if we could point to any black achievement that was
not made in the midst of a foreign society, and upon the
basis of a foreign culture—even Léopold Senghor writes
his really beautiful poetry in French!—I could be
prouder of us—"

"Harry—" Kathy said, "you mustn't! You really
mustn't—"

Harry ignored her. In fact, he didn't even hear her.
He went on, quietly.

"We have always been a fratricidal people. Today, in
Mother Africa, we slaughter each other instead of taking
on Rhodesia or the Union of South Africa, using white
mercenaries to teach us the most efficient methods of
massacring our brothers. Good thing. For having remained in the state of primitive Negroid idiocy that
made it possible for a handful of white adventurers—
stinking white bastards, of course, but with the respectable qualities of brains and guts—to dominate a whole
continent, if we tried to do something about those two
unutterable obscenities of racist swine, they would ex-
terminate us on the basis of superior technology, at
least—"

"But, 'Arree," Ouija said, "in the United States you
had, until the racist assassins murdered him, your very
great Doctor Martin Luther King, and you have the

statesman Bunche, and such beautiful men as 'Arree Belafonte and Sidney Poitier and—"

"Who are products of a white education, of a white culture, and who, precisely for that reason, don't count, Ouija, *chérie*. In America we are guilty of an even more unpardonable crime—being there at all. If our ancestors had had either brains or balls, they'd have died first. For a man who accepts slavery is like a woman who assists at her own violation by removing her panties. And what is even more unpardonable, we made *good* slaves. In three hundred years of North American slavery, there were only one hundred and twenty-five trifling, half-hearted revolts, every one of them—except Nat Turner's —betrayed by a black man to his master for a pair of cast-off boots, or a worn and faded coat. And now, having got up off our hands and knees—the proper position for being kicked in the tail, or being fornicated dog-fashion— three hundred years too late, we distinguish the worthiness of our cause by using even the deaths of our martyrs as excuses for looting and arson. And now our younger idiots are on record as demanding their own version of the segregation we were fighting against in the first place. The victim pleads guilty, *Messieurs les Juges*. I am not proud of being black . . ."

"I understand that," Ahmad Senior said soberly. "I have had much the same feeling about my own people, too, at times—"

"Your people, *mon cher vieux*," Harry said, "are triple victims. Of their climate, of their temperament, and of their religion. Chiefly of their religion, which never even hinted at the meaning of honor; that exploited lies as a justifiable strategy until now; nobody ever believes anything your leaders say. But almost as much, of your temperament, which is so ardent and so little introspective that you need only to *say* a thing to believe it. Which is why you thought you could beat the one indisputably superior race on earth today—the Jews, who have been made so by selective breeding in the Darwinian sense, because we *soi-disant* Christians killed off the weak and stupid among them in two thousand years of pogroms, leaving the tough and the smart to breed. As a people, you Arabs belong to history, and we Negroes to prehistory. Oh, hell, I—"

"Us, Harry," Kathy said. "Aren't you going to give us hell, too?"

"No. You whites have your private hell inside you. And the name of it is guilt. Or the consciousness of guilt, God pity you! So now, having talked too goddamned fornicating much, I am, Ahmad permitting, going to ride that damned cranky Arabian mare of his—"

"No!" Raoul Levi said. "Not yet! You are fabulous, 'Arry! The black philosopher. The philosopher of a decadent defeatism, as corrupt as that of Nietzsche or Schopenhauer, who believes in nothing—"

"Especially not in youth, which, as Bernard Shaw—I think—said, is wasted on the young. And certainly not that the most spoiled, pampered, soft generation in recent history can do what good men and true have tried for centuries to do, and failed. What I do believe in, *mon cher* Maoist revolutionary, is evil. That it persists. That it endures—"

"'Arree," Ouija said, getting up from her father's lap and coming over to where he sat, "you must not hate yourself, or your own people. *Tu es très beau.* The most handsome man I have known in all my life."

She bent suddenly and put her slim, golden arms about his neck.

"So do not torture yourself, *mon très cher*. And above all, do not commit the *bêtise*, the *sottise*, the stupidity of marrying this pale, insignificant little thing because her skin is white. You can marry me. Or make me *ta maîtresse. Ca m'est égal.* I love you, *tu sais.* I love you very dearly."

Harry grinned at her crookedly. Put up his hands and unwound her arms from about his neck.

"Thank you very much, dear little Ouija," he said. "And now, having insured that your father will shoot me, will you have the goodness at least to attend my funeral?"

Then he stood up and limped off in the direction of the stables.

"I think," Ouija said solemnly, "that I have been rejected. And that my heart is broken. Come and comfort me, Raoul—you filthy red swine!"

When the two of them had strolled away, Kathy got up, a little indecisively, and started after Harry. But, before she had gone two steps, she felt a hand upon her arm, and, turning, stared into Dhahaba's face.

"Do not mind her, my little daughter," Dhahaba said gently. "It is customary for young girls to fall in love with older men. She will get over it—and Harry handles these things extremely well—"

"So I see," Kathy said, and the acid note in her own voice surprised even her. "He should, shouldn't he? I mean with all the practice he's had—"

She turned then, started walking towards the stables.

"Wait!" Ahmad Senior called out. "Tell Hamid to give you Bellejour. She's a gentle creature. Some of the others, especially the geldings, aren't to be trusted . . ."

"Thank you," Kathy said. "But what I need most is a riding crop . . ."

"Not for Bellejour," Ahmad said. "She is very docile. Purebred Arab and—"

"No—to use on Harry!" Kathy said.

Chapter
Six

"Harry?" Kathy said plaintively, as they cantered the two beautiful dappled-gray Arab mares side by side down the curving bridle path under the plane trees. "Am I a pale, insignificant little thing?"

"No," Harry said. "I think you're kind of cute, honey-chile. Only you made a mistake. You never should have bailed out into this particular jungle—"

"Like that Miss Europe you told me about? You mean you're the Ibo king?"

"No. He wasn't having any, remember? And I'm buying. A fine, really stacked hunk of nothing."

She looked at him, bleakly. Pulled up her mount. Harry pulled up the frisky little gray, too.

"Don't you think I've been insulted enough for one day?" Kathy said.

"Sorry," Harry said. "Didn't mean it that way, Kathy. All I meant was, from my viewpoint at the foot of the basement stairs, this Boy Scout-style good deed is turning out to be a singularly unproductive relationship. Dead-end street, in fact."

"You don't have to go through with it," Kathy said. "I'll just have the little bastard. Go home and—"

"No," Harry said. "The South just ain't that broad-minded yet, Miss Anne. Not even Durham, Nawth Ca'linah. You'll have had it, you do that. Play it my way, baby. It'll be over before you know it, and—"

"Harry," she said, "aren't you fond of me? Not even the tiniest little bit?"

"Do you want me to be?" he said.

"Yes. Today, anyhow. My morale's shot to hell. Here, *I'm* the outcast. The—the pale, insignificant little thing!"

"Got to you, didn't she? Good Lord! It's nothing to cry over, Kathy!"

"Yes, it is," she sniffled, " 'cause it's—it's so true!"

He danced Ahmad's little mare over close to her and put his arm around her shoulder.

"Don't, Kathy," he said.

"Can't help it!" she sobbed. "Oh, Harry, I feel so—so whipped!"

He dismounted. Helped her down, too. Tied the two mares to the whitewashed picket fence. Lifted her effortlessly into the air and sat her upon the top rail. Climbed up beside her. She was still crying.

"Doesn't this road go anywhere they can't see us?" she got out. "I *hate* them! Always watching!"

"No, it doesn't," Harry said. "And you don't hate anybody, baby. You're just upset because you're out of your milieu. Should have stayed down home under the spreading magnolia tree. Or even up on the Avenue Foch. Or any place where yellow hair and blue-green eyes are all you need. Paris is a frontier town. Crossroads of the whole fornicated world. Everybody meets here, and brings some mighty fine ass-end-to ideas along. And the French—the tired, old, infinitely corrupt French— look on and grin! Paris—*la ville lumière!* Like hell it is. It's running a dead heat with New York, Rome, and London for the title of outhouse of the world—or the cesspool. I wouldn't know. Hell, baby, here the lesser breeds don't know they're lesser or even what the law is. And all 'the new caught savage peoples, half devil and half child,' look charming to jaded old European eyes. 'Specially when they've got a grin like Xuan Thuy's—"

"Kipling," Kathy said. "You read all the wrong books, didn't you? Harry—why don't you marry Ouija? She's gorgeous. And she's your kind and rich and—"

"Has claws. I'd have to beat hell out of her twice a week or she'd think I'd stopped loving her. Too much of a chore. Prefer my women civilized. And little Ouija —ain't. Should have picked her folks more carefully. Arab—and Negro. Good Lord!"

"Harry, *you're* a racist! You really are! And a traitor

to your own people. I'll bet you've never been in love with a—a colored girl in your whole life."

"Don't put your money on that one, Miss Anne. You'd lose."

"Oh," Kathy said. "What was she like?"

"Gorgeous. Diahann Carroll and Lena Horne combined. With the better features of each."

Kathy looked at him then, a long, slow, sidelong glance.

"Why didn't you marry her then?" she said.

"Tried. Tried like old hell. Got down on my knees. Begged, pleaded, cried, prayed. Only she wasn't having any—not permanently, that is—thank you mighty kindly. Thought—and told me—I was too goddamned black."

"She was a fool!" Kathy said fiercely.

"No, she wasn't, baby girl. She was a realist, that's all. Bad as they have it, light-skinned mulattoes still have it a hell of a lot better than blacks. The only thing I've never been able to forgive her for was getting rid of my—our—kid. Didn't even tell me she was knocked up. Took a train north. Chicago. Later on she married the abortionist who snatched our little bundle. Yellow bastard who looks just like a white man. Made him shed a wife and three kids for her. She could. I only hope she's happy—"

"Har—ry," Kathy said, "she wouldn't marry you—and yet, she—"

"Let me. Sure Lord did. Frequently. Of course. That was her white blood talking. Black cats are all right in the dark. Only don't be seen with 'em by daylight. You shouldn't find that strange. Just about your own slant on your Creep à la Français—"

"Harry, please!" Kathy said.

"Sorry," Harry said. "Again."

"In her place, I would have," Kathy said.

"In her place, you would have what?"

"Married you. For keeps, that is. You really are something special, Harry. Or else I wouldn't always be falling over women who're in love with you. Your cheering section, Fats calls them. Or your public relations squad. Building your image—"

"*Now,* you've said it, Miss Anne," Harry said, and his voice was bleak. "My image. Harry Forbes, the clarinetist. The jazzman who blows it low, gritty, and cool. *Me,* they don't know. Only the image. Far as I know, only two girls have been in love with me in my whole miserable life."

"Two? Fleur—and her? The one who—"

"Skipped? No. Hell, no! She just liked the way I socked it to her, that's all. Always have been pretty good in that department."

Kathy shot a sidelong glance at him. But he wasn't boasting. He was just stating a fact. A fact that was not only unimportant to him, but that he didn't even think was particularly interesting.

"Then—who?" she whispered.

"Another girl. Black girl—Miriam Makeba type. Must have had Masai ancestors. The Masai women are the most beautiful black girls on earth. Only she was from the wrong side of the tracks—"

"Harry, you don't mean—that your folks—your family—?"

"Objected? That Negroes have social classes, too? Funny how much that surprises whitefolks. Yes, Miss Anne. Both. Matty was a sweet kid, but her background was—rough. Her old man got his in a crap game when one of the players grabbed the dice and proved the old goat had pulled a switch with a new pair that was loaded. Sectioned Matty's old man's jugular and his carotid both with one swipe of an old-fashioned straight razor. After that, Matty's Ma made do by running a rooming house. Kind of a pad that has a bed in every room. Running water. Lots of towels. Sort of homey place where no questions are asked. Where the Baptist preacher could take the choir mistress and know that Matty's Ma would forget she had ever seen either of them before when she went to church next Sunday . . ."

"You could have eloped," Kathy said.

"Thought of that. Was planning to. But my Mom got there first. Some of the good ladies of Saint Mark's Episcopal Church saw me kissing Matty one night, and—"

"Harry! You're an Episcopalian? Like—me? Like my family?"

"Of course. Snobbery knows no racial lines. Goddamnit! I used to sneak down to Stokley—that was where what my Mom called 'the lowdown niggers' lived —and listen to the footwashing Baptists sing and shout. They enjoyed their religion. And could they sing! Jesus, baby, just listening to 'em would give me the shivers. That would get Mom wild. That, and my hanging around outside joints called The Bucket o' Blood and The Dirty Spoon. Outside. I didn't dare go in. You see, I was looking for my heritage. Trying to find it. And they had it—all the hustlers and crapshooters and pimps. They lived. And there I was, a skinny black kid in a neat, buttoned-up, expensive suit, trying, without even knowing it, to escape from being made into an imitation white man. Son of two college graduates. Two heroes—"

"Heroes?" Kathy said.

"Yes, goddamnit! Do you know, have you any idea what kind of brains and guts it takes for a black man or woman to get an education, make it into the middle class? To stay there? To get to be a M.D.? To pin that Master of Science in Education after your name like my Mom? To live quietly, decently in a good brick house, exercise the monumental degree of tact it takes to keep Southern black servants who feel disgraced to work for their own race? Hell, baby—I tasted soul food for the first time in my life when I already had my own band and was playing one-night stands. Watermelon, hominy grits, collard greens, chitlins, hog jowls, black-eyed peas, spareribs never entered our door. We ate white bourgeois food, menus that Mom clipped out of *Ladies Home Journal* or *McCall's*. But I was always sneaking off down to Stokley. To hear that good, great, gritty, sweaty, black-smelling music. The blues. Gospel music. Jazz. Funky music. Lyrics like 'Momma lemme squeeze your lemon 'til your love come down'—"

"Now you're exaggerating," Kathy said.

"No, I'm not. That's what the song said. Or, 'Blue-gum Woman Doncha Pizen Me.' I could hear it inside my head while the choir at Saint Mark's was singing those nice, stately, ice-cold hymns out of the Anglican hymnbook. I wanted to scream out, 'Hit it!' Throw back my head and wail—

Lord, what did I ever do
To be born so gawddamn' Black 'n Blue!'"

"Matty," Kathy said. "Tell me about her—"

"Mom went to see her. I didn't know about it until afterwards. Until it was too late. Tried to buy her off. Offered to pay her fare north with enough left over to

live until she found work. But Matty took all that long
green and threw it on the floor. But her Ma picked it
up. Said, 'Don't you worry none, Miz Forbes. Matty'll
be on the twelve-oh-five tonight—' "

"And was she?" Kathy whispered.

"Yes. And in a cathouse two months later. Her way
of getting even, I suspect. With me, Mom, her Ma, and
the world . . ."

"And you—what did you do then?"

"Went off to college like a nice, well-washed, dutiful
son. Majored in French, which was a sop for me after
all those years in Switzerland—"

"Where your mother sent you after she caught you
playing piano in a whorehouse. Harry, what an awful
liar you are!"

"That's no lie, Miss Anne. That's a fact. Oldest
hustler in the house—old battle-ax crowding fifty—taught
me the facts of life. Said to me, 'You're a big boy, Harry.
Time you got bred. Come on upstairs with me . . .' I'll
be grateful to her all the rest of my life . . ."

"Why?" Kathy said in a still, small voice.

"Taught me right. Not to be in a hurry. To relax.
That the proof of a man is that a woman enjoys herself.
First. Second. Up to three or four times before he turns
loose and gets there, too. This is a hell of a subject, isn't
it? Let's change it."

"All right," Kathy said, a little breathlessly. "Tell me
about college. Where'd you go?"

"New York University. There's where I got my letter
in track. Switched over to Juilliard in my third year.
Took my degree in composition. Told Mom I was going
to do classic music like Dean Dixon. She went for that
big. Respectable. Not lowdown niggerish like jazz. More

merde. I was sitting in with the boys of Fifty-Second Street every night. At Birdland. Uptown, too. Small's Paradise. The Apollo. Made a good living arranging for the greats. Most of 'em couldn't read—"

"You mean they actually couldn't *read?*"

"Music. The newspapers, yes. The sporting sheets— the odds on the bangtails, sure. But notes? Damned few of them. So I fell in for some loot. Lived it up a little. That was when I got mixed up with this Jewish girl. Sweet little thing. Clinging. Her old man ran a jewelry store on Sixth Avenue. He pulled Mom's stunt on me— tried to buy me off. He was right. There wasn't any future for a black boy and a white girl in the U.S.A. So I took his dough, split it in half, gave half to the NAACP, and half to the United Jewish Charities. Got signed receipts from both, stuck them in an envelope, and sent 'em to him registered mail. Then I hit the road with my boys. I'd already switched over to the pipe by then, and—hell, I'm boring you stiff."

"No, you're not," Kathy said. "Nothing about you bores me. You never have. You—frighten me. You make me madder'n old hell. You—you make me feel sort of— queer—but you *never* bore me."

"Queer-queer, or horny-queer?" Harry said, grinning at her.

"Oh, all right! I—I do wonder sometimes—what it would be like—but that's no good, is it? There's no fu- ture for—us. There can't be. You know that. Tell me, why'd you go to Vietnam?"

"Didn't know then. Now, I do. It was to prove things to myself, actually. But, back then, I blamed it on her, in part. On Deborah. This Jewish girl. You see, I'd read about her in the papers. About how she'd finally taken a stroll out of an open window. Twenty-three stories up."

"Because of—*you?*" Kathy's voice was so low that he had to read her lips.

"Hardly. Except maybe in the sense that I was an early warning of how sick she was—how sick any gray chick would have to be to go for a black boy in God's country. That was three years later. No, four. I suppose life had got to be too much for her. It had for me, baby! By then I'd been down the line, paid my dues. Already learned the jazzman's classic phrase. Somebody in Duke Ellington's band said it first, I think, while they were taking some bows down South because the good white-folks were drunk enough to clap for nigger bandmen. 'Bend, you hungry fathead, bend!' "

"Harry—" Kathy whispered.

"Too much," he went on. "Too many nights of being run out of town because some lushed-up gray chick said out loud, 'Jesus, that there black boy's good lookin'!' Too many days of riding five, six hundred miles before you could find a town with enough Negroes in it to have a colored fleabag where you could eat and sleep. Too many nights of playing to cracker cornballs who thought they were Clyde Barrow and started in to kill themselves a nigger bandman to prove it. Too damn' many Southern cops who didn't like my carefully acquired Northern accent, or the way I carried myself. Not enough downhome stoop'n shuffle, Miss Anne! Too many likkered-up white boys who thought it was great fun to run their hands up between our girl singer's legs. Too many—oh, shit! How'd I get onto *this* subject, anyhow?"

"I asked you to," Kathy said. "Harry—"

"Yes, baby girl?"

"Kiss me."

He didn't say anything. He just looked at her.

"They—they're still watching us." She pointed through a break in the trees towards one of the three tennis courts. Ouija, Raoul, Ahmad Second, and a French girl had been playing mixed doubles. But now they had all stopped and were staring towards where Harry and Kathy sat on the rail fence. From their gestures it was clear they were discussing the matter, and with considerable animation, at that.

"So?" Harry said

"We're—supposed to be—lovers, aren't we? So—let's not disappoint them. Besides—"

"Besides what?" Harry said.

"Besides, somehow, it seems I—I want you to."

He kissed her. Very gently. Expertly. With the skill of long practice. But what was there most of all was tenderness. And it was real.

He felt the tears on her face. Tasted their salt. Drew back. Looked at her.

"Oh, Harry!" she wept. "You shouldn't have! That wasn't fair! That wasn't fair at all!"

He smiled at her sadly.

"*What* wasn't fair, Miss Anne?" he said.

"To—to kiss me like that. Now I—"

"Now you—what?"

But she'd got it back. Her control. Her identity. Her conception of who and what she was. Which, Harry thought with admiration, was quite a trick.

"No," she said quietly. "It's—still—no good, Harry. So let's not confuse the issue, shall we? You're doing me a favor, I suppose. You—you've suffered enough. And so have I, now. In these last two weeks, I've made up for all my sins. So don't kiss me anymore. Not even if I ask you to. Farce is one thing. Tragedy's another. We shouldn't mix them up. Not ever. So—"

She stood up then, untied her borrowed mare. Mounted. Clapped her knees into Bellejour's flanks. Started off at a hard, pounding gallop. Harry sat there, thinking, "You fool. You fool. Now she knows."

Then he got up, mounted, and raced after her, leaning forward on the gray's neck, riding like a jockey, like a centaur, going on.

Chapter
Seven

The minute Harry saw her face as she came towards Emil's sidewalk café on the morning of that twenty-seventh day he'd known her, he knew something was wrong.

"All right," he said tiredly, "spill it, Kathy."

"I—I got a letter from Papa. Yesterday afternoon. With a check in it."

"So?" Harry said.

"He—he wants me—to come home. Right now. This minute."

"So?" Harry said again.

"He says that if I'm not there within two weeks, he's coming after me. And he will, too! Just in time to ruin everything! 'Cause already my skirts are getting tight in the waist! And I can't even get into my stretchpants anymore. And—"

Harry looked at her. Most of what she'd said was imaginary, he decided; born of fear. She wasn't showing yet. Not at all.

"How big is the check?" he said.

"Three thousand dollars. Papa's always sort of liberal with me . . ."

"Liberal? I'd call that indulgent. With that much lettuce, you can go to Sweden, Miss Anne . . ."

"Harry, I've told you and told you—"

"That you won't get rid of *l'enfant de la patrie*. That abortion is murder. I agree. I'll spend the rest of my life wondering what my kid would have been like if Milly had let him live—"

"Milly?" Kathy said.

"Millicent. The high brown I told you about. Hell of a name, isn't it? So, we go through with our little comedy?"

"Yes, Harry. Now tell me something. Will it cost an awful lot to divorce me? 'Cause if it will, I'll find some way to send you the money."

"We'll cross that bridge when we get to it. Couple of other deals I've got to figure, first. How to let myself down easy, for instance. So Ahmad won't think I'm an absolute jerk. Nor Fats and the other boys in the band.

Say, I've got it! You get a cable saying your old man's in a bad way. I'll tell Louis I'm expecting an important wire and to forward it out to Ahmad's. That's where the reception will be. Ahmad insists on that—"

Kathy looked at him. A long time. So long that before she spoke, he saw she'd made up her mind about something.

"Harry, there're direct flights to New York from Nice, aren't there?"

"Yes, Kathy. Why?"

"Ahmad's lending us one of his cars. You knew that, didn't you?"

"Yes. The Farcel Vega. So?"

"You—you don't tell them what's in that cable. You— you read it and put it in your pocket. Then—*after* you get back from the *Côte*, you show it to them. Less— shocking, that way, don't you think? Less—cruel . . ."

"Hmmmm—" Harry said. "Not bad. Finesse. A *good* put on. You're a bright girl, Miss Anne!"

"Harry—after I—I'm out of your life—marry Ouija. Do. Please do. She—she's perfect for you. And I—I do so want you to be happy!"

"Why thank you mighty kindly, Miss Anne!" Harry said. Then he saw that she was crying.

"Don't, Kathy," he said gently.

"Can't help it," she said. "I feel so—so rotten. Harry— tell me another thing. Look me straight in the face and tell me. I—I've *got* to know. Do you—do you love me?"

He looked at her. Thought: Here's where the world stops. Where I get off. Then he said it.

"Yes, Kathy."

Her chin shook. Her mouth quivered.

"Harry," she wept, "you mustn't! You—you can't! I'm awful. I'm—bad—cheap—no good. I've got—another man's baby inside me—you—you know that!"

Harry smiled at her.

"Whoever told you that what a body knows has anything to do with what a body feels, Miss Anne?"

"Ohhhhh!" she wailed. "What I said to you. My own words. Rammed back into my throat to choke on! Another thing. I—I'm a white Southerner. A—a bigot. Prejudiced. I—hate Negroes! I—I despise them!"

"The word's 'niggers,' Miss Anne," Harry said.

She bent her head. Looked up again.

"Harry—" she whispered, "you know what's *really* wrong with me?"

"Yes, girl baby. You're scared."

"And—and you know what of?"

"The mess you're in. Enough to scare tougher dames than you," Harry said. But he knew it wasn't that. The question was whether she was going to have the honesty to say it. Or the guts.

"No," Kathy said. "That's *not* it. Not entirely, anyhow. I *am* afraid of that, of course. But what—terrifies me is—"

She stopped. Turned her face away from him.

"Go on, girl baby," Harry said.

"The—the way I feel about—you," she said.

He didn't say anything. He just waited. When she spoke again, finally, she'd taken what seemed to him a new tack, unrelated to the other. Only it was neither new nor unrelated. He slid into the iron chair, next to her. Somehow, he felt he needed support.

She said quietly, "My Uncle Tony was stationed in

Africa, during the war. At a place on the Ivory Coast. And you know what he said?"

"No," Harry said. "What did your Uncle Tony say, girl baby?"

"That he got out just in time. That every day longer he stayed there, those black girls kept getting prettier and prettier. And whiter and whiter. By the time he left, the one he was—"

"Shacking up with," Harry said.

"Yes. The one he was sleeping with, had got to look just like Betty Grable!"

Harry threw back his head and laughed. It was funny, in a way. But his laughter tasted bitter in his mouth.

"Me," he said. "Whom do I look like to you, Kathy?"

"Like—you," she whispered. "That's what makes it worse."

"Visibility zero. Like the London Airport. Don't follow you, Miss Anne."

"Know you don't. You look like you. Black—and—and —just beautiful. A combination I—I didn't know could exist. That I couldn't even see, until that girl—kissed you that night. Until I saw Ouija looking at you and looking at you and looking at you, and I turned around and *saw*. What she was seeing, I mean. What was giving her that 'Don't-you-see-I'm-all-yours-please-for-God's-sake-come-*do*-something-about-it' expression. That you're special. V*ery* special. So—when we've gone through with this—this farce, I'm going to leave you right away, Harry. While I—still can. Before I mess up both our lives. You—you deserve better. And I—I'm not strong enough to stand what being a black man's wife would cost me. Harry—"

"Yes, Kathy?" The weariness was bone-deep now.

"Don't hate me. Please don't hate me. 'Cause if you did, if you do, I'll solve this another way. The way your —Deborah did—"

"Kathy—" he said.

"So, I'm asking you to—to let me live, Harry. To let me keep—all this. To—to think about nights. When everyone else is asleep. *Our* thing. Yours and mine. But mostly mine. My *special* thing. That nobody else has got. That no other girl I know down home can ever have. To keep. And hug it to my heart when they're saying mean, thoughtless things about colored pepole. You and—the little limp you walked with. The way you grinned at me— and tied me up in knots just talking. Those ideas of yours that sounded so—so weird, and turned out to be so right the minute I got a chance to think about them. Then— your music. Your music I was so damn' jealous of 'cause it was all for—her—for Fleur—funny I can't even *think* her name without hurting a little—and never for me. I wanted you so to make a piece for me. A blue, sad, laughing, crazy mixed-up song—as much like me as those bamboo fronds and temple gongs and—and butterflies and fans fluttering were—like her—"

He stared at her. He hadn't known or believed she was so perceptive.

"You heard that?" he said. "You actually did?"

"I *saw* it," Kathy said. "Made my flesh crawl. It was— so beautiful, Harry. And so awful. You, standing up there playing your heart out—and crying. But I didn't— don't—mean that much to you, I guess—"

"I don't know how much you mean to me, Kathy," Harry said gently. "I wasn't given—time."

But she had gone away from him then; far away into some deep recess of her mind.

"Harry, how soon can you make the arrangements?" she said.

"With any luck, starting today—about a week."

"Good," she said. "I'll still be all right, then."

"All right for what?" he said.

She turned to him, and made an impish face.

"You'll see, *mon très cher et si beau* 'Arree," she mocked, imitating Ouija's accent and tone of voice perfectly. "I am *certaine* of it!"

But the very next night, it so happened, was Friday, May 10, 1968: the night all hell broke loose in Paris, city of light, capital of *la Belle France,* mother of modern European civilization.

Harry didn't see the start of it. He and Fats had already left the little flat they'd shared on the Rue Benoît ever since Harry had loaned his own place on the Rue Monsieur le Prince near the Carrefour de l'Odéon to Kathy. They'd noticed, of course, as they walked towards the nearest Métro station—Odéon itself—that the students were gathering. But they paid little attention to that. The students had been out in force every night since May 6, the day the leaders of the riot at the Sorbonne had been jailed. And they had a natural tendency to underestimate the students, who, they were sure, had never had it rough, hadn't yet paid their dues to life in terms of suffering, had never been down the line.

"Young jerks!" Fats snorted. Afterwards, Harry was to remember that phrase.

By the time it really got started, Harry was on the bandstand. He'd just finished a solo: one of his set pieces, a thing he was already famous for among Paris' jazz connoisseurs, "Rainy Night Blues," which *Le Jazz Hot* freely predicted was going to become a classic, and the audience's response had been unusually warm. So he decided to try his new composition, to see how it would go, as a precaution, maybe, to get it right, before he played it for—her.

"And now, all you dear sweet people," he said in English first, because it was the thing to do, because in Paris that gave the whole thing style, authenticity, chic, "a new little thing of mine. It's called 'Little Girl Lost: A Song for Kathy.'" But nowadays, since outrageous prices, the Gaullist policy of hostility towards the Anglo-Saxon bloc, and the natural rudeness of the French had ruined the tourist business beyond repair, most of the faces in the crowd remained blank, so he said it over again: "*Et maintenant, mes très chers amis, une composition toute neuve. C'est à moi, bien entendu. Je l'appelle 'Petite Fille Perdue: Une Chanson pour Kathy . . .'*"

He tilted his head back and ripped out the first few bars of "Dixie." Then he started to play with that, making variations on the theme, shading it off into a new thing, in a sort of lap dissolve in five bars, so that "Dixie" was gone by the middle of them, and the new theme was there. The music was limpid, pure; he poured sunlight into it, rippled laughter through it, marched in a parade of rag dolls, teddy bears; let them hear a baby girl prattling, skipping rope, singing. Then it darkened. That blue strain crept into it, twining serpentinely around the beat, not exactly contrapuntal but somehow opposing the theme, threatening to work it some hurt, then rising, rising, drowning the sunlight, darkening the laughter, going atonal, cacophonic, harsh, the way confusion always is. Momentarily, he brought the sunlight back, the joy, as if to demonstrate that the loss of girl-hood, of innocence, is no sudden thing; but always spiraling about the main theme, just one beat off, half a note behind it, that darker sound came, febrile, feverish with sensuality now, shot through with a wilder strain, the clink of champagne glasses, and the clarinet sobbing the words "No, no, no" endlessly until it broke upon one last "No!" that was a desperate shriek, a scream. After that, the song was all blues, a little girl's crying, a wail of desolation, loss, and pain. You could hear her groping, hands up and out to find the sun, to reach the land you can't go back to, recapture innocence irre-vocably lost, to put bleak knowledge away from her, to reject the night. Only she couldn't. No one ever can.

What he blew now was defeat; a long, long dying line, so soft . . . slow . . . bitter . . . sad . . . resigned that the silence was there and echoing before they knew he'd done with it.

He lowered the clarinet. There was no sound. Not even the rasp of breathing. No one clapped. No one cheered.

But at a nearby table, quite suddenly, a girl buried her face in her hands and cried.

He heard Fats' breathy groan. "Jesus, boy! Too great. Too goddamn great. You can't do this to people. You can't. They don't come to this clip joint to have their guts ripped out of 'em. That last line now. No, six bars back. Play it again. I want to hear how you did that. It ain't possible. I know I heard it, but I still don't be-lieve—"

And it was then that Jean Claude, the waiter, came up to him.

"*Ta fiancée,* 'Arree," he said. "*Au téléphone.* She has fear. *Très peur. A moi—ça semble qu'elle est hystérique . . .*"

Harry put down the clarinet. Limped to the phone. Picked it up.

"Harry!" her voice came over to him, vibrant, shrill, metalic. "I'm in the Drugstore! The one on St. Germain! I—I can't get home! They're—they're killing people. They're bringing them in here—all bloody! It's awful! The police are shooting and clubbing people, and the students are digging up the paving stones—"

He heard through the phone the crash of glass breaking, the eerie, echoing-after tinkling of the slivers showering down.

"Kathy!" he got out. "Kathy, baby girl, are you all right?"

"So far," she wailed. "Somebody just threw a paving stone through the store window. Oh, Harry, I'm so damned scared! Can you come get me? Can you?"

"Hold on, baby," he said, prayerfully. "Be there in a minute."

But it took him the better part of an hour. The taxi entered the boulevard at the nearer end, crossing the Seine over the Pont de la Concorde. But at the intersection of St. Germain and the Rue des Saints-Pères, the cab driver jammed on his brakes.

"Pay me," he said. "Then march yourself. *File. Futez moi le champ.* I've a wife and three kids, Mister. If it is that you wish to commit suicide, *à moi ça met égal. Je m'en fiche.* You can do it walking. *Là bas, c'est beaucoup trop dangereux!*"

Harry paid him.

"*J'ai une femme, moi aussi,*" he said gently. "*Mais, étant donné qu'elle est là bas, il faut que j'y m'en aille—*"

"*Dommage,*" the taxi driver said. "*A pity. Mais* this old heap is my livelihood, and *ma femme et mes trois gosses* have need of me. I wish you *bonne chance*. If you do find *la vôtre* with her head unsmashed, make a long detour, walking, and come out by the Pont Sully on the other end. That is if you can cross the Boule Mich' at all. There are ten thousand *étudiants enragés* there, and three thousand CRS, trying mutually to kill each other. *Tant pis*, they don't succeed. Then, *peut-être*, we'd have some peace . . ."

Harry started off down the boulevard, walking. But it was no good to go that way, and he knew it. From where he was, he could already hear the cough of the grenade launchers, and now and again a windblown whiff of tear gas stung his eyes. He could hear a confused babble of shouts, screams of pain, shrieked obscenities. He could see the CRS now—the *Compagnies Républicaines de Sécurité*—the meanest, roughest, most brutal riot cops on the face of God's green earth. They wore gas masks. They were wading into the students, using their *matraques* on them. Harry could hear those yard-long clubs crunching against supposedly intellectual skulls. Or rather against the motorcycle helmets most of the students wore to protect their heads. The *enragés* were using ax handles—bought for the occasion—on *les flics*. Paving stones. Some of them were shooting *fronds lance-pierres*, slingshots with thick rubber bands cut from the inner tubes of the dozens of cars they'd already wrecked. But they weren't using rocks in their slingshots. They were using ball bearings, also bought for the occasion.

Billes d'acier, ball bearings, in a slingshot, turn it into a deadly weapon. Almost as effective, at close range, as a gun.

He could see Les Deux Magots, now. It was crowded with CRS. They were massing for a charge. Then he saw what they were going to attack. *Le Drugstore*, directly across the boulevard. Where Kathy was.

The burning cars, and the Molotov cocktails the students in front of the Drugstore were throwing in the direction of the police, turned night into day, even though all the streetlamps had been smashed by then. The CRS were firing their "trombones," grenade launchers, and the air was white with tear gas. But Harry didn't hesitate. He jerked the handkerchief out of his breast pocket and tied it over his nose and mouth. Then in his hopping, skipping cripple's run, he came straight towards the Drugstore, jumping the pooled flames of the gasoline-filled bottles, ducking the whistling *billes d'acier*, the flying paving stones, bent over, running low, zigzagging like the trained veteran he was, having neither the time nor the breath for fear. A bolt with the nut still on it grazed his cheek, opening it almost to the bone. He came on, the blood soaking his handkerchief, until some-one cried out:

"Hold! It's not a flic. *C'est un Noir.* One of ours, probably!"

Which was what saved him. There were many Africans from the emerging countries among the students. He got there, gasped out:

"*Merci, mes gars! Avez-vous vu une petite blonde, qui—*"

Then abruptly, Kathy was in his arms.

"Oh, you're hurt!" she sobbed. "You're bleeding!

You're bleeding something awful! My fault! Always my fault! I've made you get yourself halfway killed for me, and—"

"Shut up, baby," Harry said. "Come on!"

He dragged her out of the Drugstore and raced with her down a side street. But the taxi driver's estimate was no exaggeration. There were thousands of students, and almost as many police. Every way they turned they found their way blocked by barricades, most of them blazing. The gutters were orange-red with burning gasoline, capped by sooty smoke. They could hear the tanks of the parked cars exploding now.

Then a hand reached out and clutched his arm.

"Follow me, 'Arry," a voice said. "I will get you and *ta 'tite* Kathy through—"

Harry turned and saw Raoul Levi. The boy had a bloodstained bandage about his head. He was red-eyed, staggering from loss of blood, from fatigue. But the grin, that infuriating and very gallant grin, never left his face.

And get them through he did. Everyone knew him, it seemed. He was one of *les héros*, only a little less important than Cohn-Bendit, himself. They'd call out, "Open up! *Ouvrez pour Raoul et ses amis!*" and the lines would part and let them pass, then close again behind them. Raoul led them to a dingy apartment building on the Rue Guisar. He unlocked the front door, went ahead of them up the filthy, foul-smelling stairs, saying gaily:

"*Suivez-moi, mes enfants!*"

They came to a cubbyhole under the roof. It had only a bed and a washbasin in it. There was no room for a chair. Books were piled up on the bed, on the floor, on shelves. The room reeked of sweat. Of unwashed male.

"My place," Raoul said. "Like it?"

"My God!" Harry said.

"Did you think I was rich, 'Arry, Black Priest of the Bourgeoisie? There are many days I don't eat. That way I can buy books. I prefer to feed my spirit rather than my belly—"

"You're not poor," Harry said slowly. "The poor don't get into the Sorbonne. Nor Nanterre."

"True. But I have cut myself off from *mes parents, qui sont très riches.* I have no longer even an allowance from *mon père.* He thinks thus to force me to return to his benevolent paternal domination. He is a big jackass, *mon père—*"

"Raoul—" Harry said, "why do you do this?"

"Because, *mon cher,* I do not like the world you old ones have made. You know why we burn cars? Because they, *les voitures,* are the symbol of crass materialism. I should love to be the slave of *une si jolie petite blonde* like your Kathy. Willingly I should kiss her feet. But I will not be the slave of the payments by installments on a refrigerator. I will not mortgage my life to buy a TV set on which I can only listen to Papa de Gaulle saying, '*Français, Françaises!* Do as I tell you! Hold still so I can screw you up the *derrière* with my flaccid old truc—' "

In spite of herself, Kathy was smiling, now.

"I will not gear my life to a consumer economy, to created needs. Nor, *ma chère petite* Kathy, who, even after hours in that crowd still smells nice, do I wish my *femme* to be enslaved by the cosmetics industry. I'd rather that she didn't shave her armpits, and that she stank a little, as a healthy she-animal should—"

"What do you want to do?" Harry said. "What, really, Raoul?"

"Wear flowers in my hair. Read Baudelaire. Sleep with all the beautiful women, including your Kathy. Be happy. Work enough to eat, but not more. Make it possible for the sons of workers to enter the Sorbonne. But a *new* Sorbonne, transformed into something more than a *usine de la mémoire,* a memory factory where *vielles barbes* lecture, lecture, lecture over facts so dead they stink like old fish in *les Halles.* A university where intelligence that doubts and questions can succeed, instead of one that turns out every year a flood of idiots with photographic memories and no capacity for thought at all. In short, I'd insure justice—in the university, and in the world. Make peace. Own nothing—except books, except paintings, sculptures which have no other use but to delight the eye, the mind. Walk in the sun. Laugh. End racism, capitalism, bigotry, religion. Bring in true Communism, the heroic Communism of Mao, instead of that quasi-capitalist *merde* of Moscow. See that everyone has enough to eat, enough beauty surrounding him, enough love. That's all. Now tell me, what do you think of *mon programme, mon cher?*"

"That, apart from the infantile stupidity of persisting in your worship of Chairman Mao who is in the forefront of the world's great mass murderers, I hope you achieve it," Harry said. "For it is very fine."

Raoul stared at him. Then he saw that Harry meant it.

"*Merci, mon cher,*" he said solemnly. "And now, not being *un voyeur,* I go. Make good use of my little bed. It is not very clean, but the springs are strong. They squeak so beautifully!"

"Raoul," Kathy said, "don't go! You're sick, hurt, and out there—"

"Are my enemies. The foes of human liberty. Who must be beaten, *ma chérie*. Do not worry about me. If you and Ouija will weep a little for me, it will be good to die. *Salut*, 'Arry, Kathy! Enjoy yourselves! I go—"

When he had gone down the stairs, Kathy looked at Harry.

"Harry," she said, her voice high, tight, edgy. "Get me out of here!"

Harry looked at her face. Her mouth. Then he sighed, "All right, Kathy . . ." And the two of them went back down the stairs.

They spent the night in the Luxembourg Gardens. They had to climb the iron fence to get in, because all the gates were shut and locked. They sat on a park bench on the Rue Guynemer side, about as far as they could get from the Boulevard St. Michel which borders on the other side of the park. It was quiet in the Gardens, because the main battle was confined to the areas where St. Germain crosses St. Michel and the Rue St. Jacques, although some particularly bloody fighting took place on the Rue Gay-Lussac as well. Harry tried to persuade Kathy that it was safe enough to climb the fence on the north side of the Gardens and come out on the Rue de Vaugirard, which crosses Monsieur le Prince, where his flat was, just before it gets to St. Michel again. But she wouldn't hear of it.

And because he knew why—that she was afraid to spend the night in the flat alone, but even more afraid of spending it within the confines of four walls where there was a bed available with him—he fell silent. The cut on his face had crusted over and was stuck to his handkerchief. It ached dully. But his right leg, after all the running and walking and climbing fences, didn't merely ache; it hurt like hell.

He put down his two hands and began to massage it; but before he'd even begun to knead the soreness out of it, Kathy was off the bench and kneeling before him. She pushed his pant's leg up to his knee and began to rub his knotted calf for him with her soft, slim, unaccustomed hands.

"Get up," he said harshly. "You're not Fleur. Not your style, Kathy. Leave me be, will you?"

She got up at once and sat down on the bench as far away from him as she could get. Then he saw how her thin shoulders were shaking, so he put out his arm and drew her to him.

"Forgive me, girl baby," he said.

"Forgive you?" she sobbed. "*You*, Harry? After I almost got you killed? And then I was too big a coward to stay in Raoul's room with you, 'cause—"

" 'S all right, baby," he said, not wanting to hear it, not now, in the present state of his defenses which were all down, trying to shut her up before she made him hate—not her, because that was no longer possible—but himself, a state of mind all too easily arrived at when he considered all he'd done and suffered for her sake, how little dignity he was displaying now, what an absolute penury of pride.

But she went on, recklessly.

" 'Cause I knew I—I'd have let you. 'Cause I *wanted* you so damn' bad. *Not* past tense. Want. Ever since— that Sunday at Ahmad's I've been crazy, sick, wild—"

He sat there in the semidarkness, frozen.

"—and it wouldn't have been—right. You see that, don't you, Harry? Not in that stinking, filthy little hole. It wouldn't have been—beautiful. Nor at your place, either."

"Then where would it be beautiful, Kathy?" he said.

"Nowhere, tonight. Because you wouldn't know why. And I wouldn't, either. My nerves are screaming. I feel like throwing up. Making love would probably help. Only that's an awfully poor reason for making love, isn't it? I couldn't—insult you like that. Or myself, either. I wouldn't, couldn't, can't, won't, dirty what's between us now by grabbing you like a panting little bitch 'cause—"

"You're scared—and the world's been turned upside down. Again," Harry said. Then, "Thanks, baby—"

"Thanks?" she said. "Lord God, Harry! For what?"

"For getting out of there. For not leaving me—with another wound that wouldn't heal. Now put your head on my shoulder. Try to sleep . . ."

Dutifully, she did. But a little later, she said,

"The students—Harry, they—they're fighting like lions! But for what? Tell me that, lover? For what?"

He stiffened a little. She had never called him 'lover' before. Nor anything else with the slightest hint of tenderness in it. But she can now, he thought bitterly. In a little over a week she'll be on a plane . . .

"For—dreams," he said. "For a world that never was and never will be. For a cloud-cuckoo land straight out of Aristophanes. *The Birds*. Ha! For the birds, at that! They're so goddamned young that they've got their mental cherries, still. They believe in the possibility of improving society, in the perfectibility of man. Don't know, can't even see, that what's wrong with any system —Marxism, Leninism, Stalinism, Trotskyism, Maoism, Castroism, capitalism, socialism, democracy, Negritude, Black Power, Apartheid, the Church—is that ultimately they have to be run not by angels, but by men. A built-in guarantee that the works are going to get screwed up. And not necessarily out of pure cussedness, baby. Starry-eyed idealism can do a mighty good job of mounting the world dog-fashion, as Raoul and his little friends have proved tonight. Now, damnit, go to sleep! Tomorrow I'm going to take you out to Ahmad's. To stay for the duration. Because I've a hunch that this isn't going to be over all that soon. Out there, you'll be safe and—"

"No!" Kathy said. "Not Ahmad's, Harry!"

"Why not, baby?"

"Because of Ouija. I'd end up clawing her eyes out, so help me! That is, if she doesn't cut *my* throat, first. She hates me enough to. Or maybe you *enjoy* having your women fight over you?"

"The women I haven't got," Harry said.

"Harry, you're wrong," Kathy said. "On both counts. But anyhow—"

"It's got to be Ahmad's. I haven't anyplace else. This burg has gone straight to hell. It's bound to get worse before it gets better. So—"

"So, you're right. I'll be good, lover. Won't engage in an old-fashioned hairpulling contest with her. I promise you that. Besides, going out there does have one advantage, anyhow—"

"Which is?" Harry said.

"Keeps me out of the reach of temptation. No—that's

not true. Removes the possibility of my giving way to— to my carnal nature, shall we call it?" Kathy said. "Or my love for you. Or something. Anyhow—"

"Lord! Will you please, please, please, shut up and go to sleep?" Harry said.

Chapter Eight

"Of course you may bring the little Kathy *chez moi*," Ahmad said at once. "Dhahaba and I would be delighted to have her with us. She is a dear, sweet little thing. But there is one thing I must inform you, *mon cher*—or rather, two . . ."

"Which are?" Harry said.

"That I cannot guarantee absolutely her safety, there. That she will be safer at our place than she is at yours in the middle of the *Quartier Latin*, where a paving stone thrown by an *enragé* or a policeman's *matraque* may crush her poor little cranium at any minute, I grant you. But there does exist a certain danger. Remote, but nonetheless real . . ."

Harry waited. Ahmad seemed to be groping, searching his mind for the least painful way possible of saying what he had to.

"I am thinking of closing the house," he went on, "sending Dhahaba and the children to Switzerland. Of course, that presents no problem. The little Kathy can go with them—that is, if you have not married her by then . . ."

"As bad as that, Ahmad?" Harry said.

"As bad as that," Ahmad said. "Tell me, do you know—have you any idea *who* are among the groups occupying the Sorbonne?"

"*Les Katangais?*" Harry said. His voice tightened up on him, saying that name.

"They, too," Ahmad sighed. "Those miserable mercenary assassins whom we and the Belgians so thoughtfully rescued from getting their just deserts in the Congo. But I wasn't referring to them. I mean—El Fatah."

"In the *Sorbonne?*" Harry said.

"In the Sorbonne. Some of them may be students from the Arabic countries, of course. But I doubt that. What I do know is that when the last threatening telephone call I got was traced—all incoming calls to my house and the office are now traced as a matter of course now, Harry—it came from a pay booth on the Rue Gay-Lussac—"

"Anyone could pass through a street, enter a phone booth—"

"No. They are there. *L'Humanité* printed the news.

They found it strange, as good doctrinaire Communists, that our so-very-leftish students, our Cohn-Bendits, our Levis, can find room in their bastion for their worst enemies. So do I. Especially since El Fatah's local branch of thugs has taken up the sport of wrecking Jewish stores, and beating Jewish passersby into insensibility even here in the streets of Paris . . ."

"I thought you approved of that," Harry said.

"*Merde!*" Ahmad said. "I do *not!* as you should know, Harry. I don't like the Jews, but I don't advocate killing them. In fact, all my troubles stem from the fact that at a banquet for King Hussein during his recent visit to Paris, I openly advocated the kind of accommodation between us and them that you Americans seem to be arriving at with the Russians. For, if we'd allow them to teach us to do with our lands what they've done with that miserable strip of sand and rock they stole from us, many of our problems would be solved. But, being Arabs, we can only howl like the desert wolves we are—for blood. The very next day, after my—indiscretion—it started up again. The phone calls, the threats. You know, the phone rings and rings, but when anyone at home answers, there is—silence. Or obscenities screamed in Arabic and French. Ouija answered the other day, and they said to her in pure, classic Arabic: 'We will have of thee, O Desert Rose, thy virginity first, before we cut thy throat!' "

"My God!" Harry said.

"Amen," Ahmad said. "You know they tried to abduct my little Hagib. What if they were to—kidnap—Ouija? Or Ahmad Second. Or—"

"Kathy," Harry said bleakly, "if I bring her out to your house."

"They will only do that if they find out she is an heiress. I hardly think they will connect her so quickly with Les filter tip Nichols, is it not so? That's why I say the danger is remote. Bring her. I will assign the biggest, ugliest, and roughest of *mes gorilles* to protect her. I only warned you of the possibility because it seemed to me fair to do so . . ."

"Ahmad," Harry said, "why don't you just pay the bastards off?"

"Because they are Arabs," Ahmad sighed. "And I know, instructed by my own sins, that my people have no sense of measure. Aside from the fact that I violently object to contributing to an arms fund which will only insure the renewal of a war that we cannot possibly win, I know what would happen if I agreed to pay El Fatah. They would become insatiable. They would leave me penniless, my children in the street, and cut my throat *en tout cas* when they found I had no money left—"

"I see," Harry said. "How long will it be before Dhahaba *et tes gosses* leave?"

"Unhappily, it will take me all of ten days to make the arrangements," Ahmad said. "To close a house involves more than merely turning a key in a lock, *tu sais*, Harry . . ."

"That's time enough. I have to marry Kathy before ten days are out, anyhow," Harry said.

"Aha!" Ahmad said delightedly. "You mean you have been hasty?"

"I don't mean a damned thing," Harry said. "You figure it out, Ahmad. If there were only some way of cutting all the red tape so we could get married within the week and head south—"

"But there *is, mon cher.* The Mayor of Saint-Cloud is a personal friend of mine. I will call him tonight . . ."

"Ahmad," Harry said solemnly, "if you were only a little prettier, I'd kiss you, so help me!"

"Have Kathy do that, instead, and I will consider myself sufficiently rewarded. Now, if you like, I will send Muhammad to your place for her, to bring her here. Then, after the show tonight, we can all drive out to Les Granges and—"

"No," Harry said. "Tell Muhammad to drive her straight out there. Now. At once. Please. The whole *quartier* is seething. The CRS were—well—unnecessarily rough the other night. Now the students are comparing them to the Nazi SS, and De Gaulle to Hitler. I don't like the feel of things. The Government seems confused. Pompidou was in Afghanistan when most of it happened. Didn't get back until day before yesterday, the eleventh, wasn't it? And now he is granting the *enragés* too many concessions too fast—"

"I have fear that in this you have reason," Ahmad said. "We are in for it, *mon cher. Une vrai révolte—non, une révolution.* This general strike the workers have called for today—the thirteenth—are you superstitious, Harry?"

"No," Harry said.

"Nor I. But how long is it to last, *ce grève générale?* Twenty-four hours? A week? A month? Who knows? The Communists are entering upon the scene, despite the fact the students despise them as not being far enough left—as *vieilles barbes*—"

"Everyone over thirty is a 'has been' to the students," Harry sighed. "When I talk to Levi, he makes me feel a thousand years old. Still—"

"Still, *everything* is wrong in France, *aujourd'hui, mon cher*," Ahmad said quietly. "Prices are too high, wages too low. And that senile old fool in the Elysée must spend our life's blood on *sa force de frappe*—which consists of obsolete atomic bombs carried in aircraft that compared to your country's and Russia's ballistic missiles are like the caravels of Columbus. They would all be shot down before they crossed our frontiers, I am sure of it. Beyond that, *le très grand et trop vieux* Charles pours out fortunes into the French-speaking, newborn Negro republics that are, as you pointed out, run by corrupt and venal idiots. Inexperienced idiots, at that—"

"He is a great man, Ahmad," Harry said. "With all his faults, he is a very, very great man."

"*Mais oui!* That is what makes him so dangerous, Harry! Even his errors are outsized, gigantic. This business of embracing our enemies, the Communist—with the whole country headed straight for *l'enfer*, you think he will put off his trip to Roumania? You think so, Harry?"

"No. He'll go all right," Harry said.

"*Oui, mais certainement.* And he will go on insulting and injuring the allies who enriched French soil with the bodies of their sons instead of—"

"*Merde*," Harry said. "That was geography, Ahmad, not friendship. You know of any way of getting into Germany from the west without crossing France? Especially when due consideration is given to the fact that Hitler already held Scandinavia, Holland, Belgium, and Italy? Besides, *notre grand* Charles' dislike for the Anglo-Saxon bloc isn't his fault. It was Roosevelt's and Churchill's. They didn't brown-nose him properly—"

"Oh you!" Ahmad said. "Your sense of humor is blacker than your skin! I don't understand you, Harry."

"Because I am a realist," Harry said. "And reality is so sad that it is funny. When one looks at it, one must laugh—or weep. I prefer laughter. Now I have to get back to work. When will you have word from your friend the mayor?"

"Tomorrow," Ahmad said. "I will let you know tomorrow, surely—"

Tomorrow, May 14, when it had become both today and yesterday, as tomorrows always do, was, Harry realized, looking back upon it from another flickering cinema frame in time, not only the day he got the news that was to wrench his life out of its normal context, almost out of relevancy with his world, but also the day the workers of the CFDT, the *Confedération Française et Démocratique du Travail*, seized the Renault Automobile Factory at Cleón, holding the directors as hostages, and thus really started the French Republic on its long slide to the edge of disaster. But, even so, even at that, the student *enragés* were ahead of them, for the infuriated ones had seized l'Odéon, that ancient and honorable temple of the dramatic arts, the day before, proceeding to turn it into a permanent "happening" as they had already done at the Sorbonne, so now they had two places where everybody and anybody could come and shout his head off, expressing ideas that ranged from merely mediocre, through the truly brilliant, to the absolutely insane. Or to couch himself with his girl in one of the lodges—for they had scribbled on the walls along with misquoted, mistranslated quotations from Chairman Mao, and slogans damning everybody, the fine phrase, "Make your desires realities"—if he felt so in-clined. Naturally, human nature—especially French hu-man nature, Harry added wryly—being what it is, quite a few felt so inclined. And that fourteenth was also the day that De Gaulle, with his Olympian contempt for mere humanity, departed France on his state visit to Roumania.

But the minute Harry saw the grin on Ahmad's face, he knew it was going to be all right.

"*Ca marche!*" Ahmad said. "*C'est fait, mon brave!* For the sixteenth. Of course you must take the little Kathy to the *mairie aujourd'hui même* to sign ten mil-lion papers. My own physician, Moreau, will make the blood tests, and give you the results by tomorrow morning. I have ordered him to find neither *les maladies sociales* nor insanity—"

"That last one I wouldn't bet on," Harry said. "I ever tell you you're a prince, Ahmad?"

"No. And don't. Today I am so happy I might believe you. March yourself, Harry! You have much to do . . ."

When Kathy heard the news, even her lips went white. She sat down, abruptly.

She sat there, staring at him a long, long time, before she whispered, "Harry—no! I can't! We mustn't! It isn't fair to *use* you this way. It's too damned rotten and I—"

"Come on, Miss Anne, snap out of it," Harry said.

And then, quite suddenly, she was very calm. The indecision, the fear, were gone—and a look of ice-cold, desperate resolution had taken their place. She had made up her weird little mind about something, Harry saw. And that something, whatever it was, would be carried out though the CRS, the students, and all the assorted hosts of hell stood in her way. She had that

dead-game fighter's look in her eyes again. And beyond
that, something else: a stern, ruthless even, aspect
of taking herself in hand, facing what she was, and
what she had to be; defining—although he didn't know
that then, though he was not to find it out until later—
in her own terms, giving them absolute relevancy, those
eternally suspect words, integrity and honor. Seeing
her then, a long-forgotten line from Edna Millay rose
up and echoed hollowly through his mind: "And what's
to do must with dispatch be done—" *

And would be. For all the wrong reasons. The worst
of it was that he could only compound disaster by set-
ting them right. But to that end was he born; and the
principle of ribald, mocking, malicious mischief in the
universe that men call fate had so ordered it.

He took her by the arm.

"Come on, girl baby, time's a-wasting," he said.

All the fourteenth was spent wrestling with French
bureaucracy. Even with Monsieur le Maire on their side
it proved exhausting; but by night they had won, having
accomplished in one day what ordinarily would have
taken a minimum of two weeks. On the Fifteenth,
Harry rested, except that the boys in the band, Fats
Winkler, string bass, Buzz Merlin, piano, Otis Hatfield,
drums and xylophone—for Harry himself completed the
quartet by doubling on saxophone and clarinet—threw
a stag party for him at which they all got drunk, ribald,
bawdy-tongued and sentimental at one and the same
time.

"T'morrow night," Buzz rumbled, "Ol' Harry's gonna

* *Fatal Interview:* Sonnet VI

make up for every poor spade they ever hung up by his
balls for looking sidewise at a piece o' gray tail in
Georgia . . ."

Harry sat there, frozen suddenly, every drop of
whiskey fumes blasted out of his head by that phrase.

"G'wan, man!" Otis laughed. "Bet he can't. Betcha
five hundred francs he can't even get it up. Georgia
boy like him. They brainwashed him when he was a
kid. White is right—black stay back! When he sees
that cute lil' box with nothing on it 'cept a lil' yellow
hair, he's gonna fall down 'n faint!"

Then Fats saw Harry's face.

"Cool it, you cats," he said. "You're getting to m'boy.
Ain't no sense making him jumpy ahead o' time. Don't
mind 'em, soul brother. Just you go right ahead 'n be
happy. Kathy's a sweet lil' thing. Dug her the first night
she blew in here. 'Course she was brought up all wrong,
but what Southern gray chick ain't? But she's tryin'.
Really tryin'. Go easy on her, boy. She'll learn. 'Cause
she wants to, now. What I can't figure yet is whether
she *knows* she wants to or not—but you done got to
her, soul brother, 'n that's a natural fact . . ."

"Thanks, Fats," Harry said.

"For what, Harry?"

"For taking the heat off. These characters were hitting
a little too close to home. How do I know if it's Kathy
I want—or something they sold me in a perfume ad? If
you dragged her out and double-dipped her, would I go
for her still?"

"Harry," Otis Hatfield said, serious now, a note of
hurt in his voice, a hint of anger, "first time I ever saw
you, you was with your Madame Butterfly. All right, all
right, she was the greatest! That ain't what I mean.

But you tell me one little thing, boy. You *ever* go for a spade chick? 'N I don't mean no lightskin babe damn near passing for colored. I mean a spade chick so black she burns you. You ever?"

"Yes," Harry said.

"What happened?" Buzz Merlin said.

"Nothing," Harry said. "I went off to college, and she wouldn't or couldn't wait. One of those things."

That wasn't the truth. The truth was what he'd told Kathy. But you didn't tell boys like Otis and Buzz that kind of truth. They came from the same mudsill subworld that Matty had—or worse, since they were products of Harlem's asphalt jungle—and they'd had it rough enough, long enough, without his adding gratuitous injury.

"Funny," Otis said slowly. "When I was a young boy back home, I used to dream about climbing into the hay with chicks like your Kathy. Now I don't think I'd take on a gray chick permanent. No offense meant, Harry! You're different. Hell, the way you was brought up, you're practically a black whiteman. But a lot's happened since then. Different scene, nowadays. Notice how the chicks, the for-real, honest-to-God chicks, have quit straightening their hair?"

" 'I am black, but comely, O ye daughters of Jerusalem, as the tents of Kedar, as the pavilions of Solomon,' " Harry murmured. " 'Look not upon me because I am black, because the sun has burnt me. My brothers mutter against me; they put me to guard the vineyards; but my own vineyard I have not kept!' "

And suddenly the tears stood and glittered in his eyes.

"Jesus, boy," Buzz said. "Don't take on over it! By the way, what *was* that thing you said?"

"Hell, that's in the Good Book, Buzz!" Otis said. "Ain't you never been to church?"

"Yeah. But I spent so much time peeping up under the frocks of the chicks in the choir that I never did hear what the preacher said. For real, Harry—that's in the *Bible*?"

"Yes," Harry said.

"Way I figger it," Otis went on with drunken gravity, "ain't nobody ever done anything 'til they've got themselves some pride. And them kids back home, they've got it, brother! Wearing African threads, letting their hair kink the way the Lord give it to 'em. Standing up 'n fighting instead of going down on their hands and knees and waving their black asses in the air for the Man to kick the way our folks have been doing for over three hundred years. Proud of them kids, 's fact. Damn' proud."

"Sometimes I feel like a shit," Buzz said. "We run out, all of us. Took a powder. Over here in gay Paree, blowin' a real beat for cats what ain't got one idea what we're tryin' to say. Ain't got soul. Can't have it, being Frenchies and white. But I oughta be with them kids, ripping the place apart. Standin' tall . . ."

"Too late," Fats sighed. "We're old whiskers like the French kids say. Still, I'd kind of like to make the scene back home, one day—"

"When I come back from my honeymoon," Harry said suddenly, "I'll get us time off from Ahmad. Write Phil Klein in New York. Get him to arrange us a tour. New York. Chicago. 'Frisco; Los Angeles . . ."

"Atlanta?" Buzz mocked. "Durham, North Carolina, with lil' Kathy on your arm?"

Harry bent his head. Looked up again.

"No," he said. "But maybe—without her."

Fats Winkler bent close to him then, peered into his face with real concern.

"Harry," he said, "this wedding bit—is it for real? Or is it some kind of a put on? I get the damnedest feeling sometimes—"

Harry smiled at him.

"It's a real put on, Fats," he said. "Like—life."

Then he got up and walked out of there.

Kathy didn't even have that one day of rest. Dhahaba took her shopping for a wedding dress. And Ouija went along. She was genuinely helpful, displaying a taste and a flair for what was really right for Kathy that were little short of astonishing. And she was absolutely correct, in the French sense: polite, distant, cold. She was not openly antagonistic. But when it was all done, she caught Kathy by the arm and deliberately slowed her pace until Dhahaba had drawn ahead of them. Then she said, very quietly:

"You will please tell Harry that when he has demonstrated to himself that this *bêtise* you two are committing tomorrow—equally a *bêtise* for you, Kathy, because he is as wrong for you as you are for him—can never march, I shall be waiting. All my life, *s'il le faut. Et maintenant, je vous souhaite bonne chance!*"

At the *mairie*, that next afternoon, Ahmad Second stood beside his mother and Ouija. Behind them were Fats, Buzz, and Otis, and their current girl friends. Fats' date was French, but Buzz' and Otis' were Negro girl students from Dakar. Harry wondered suddenly, bleakly, if they hadn't brought the black girls along as a sort of rebuke to him for his lack of racial loyalty. Then Kathy came through a side door on Ahmad's arm, and his breath stopped. She was, in that strange, sad, mixed-up, crazy moment, absolutely glorious.

She had on a big picture hat that probably had more material in it than her wedding dress, a white lace, see-through minirobe so short that—as she told him, after-wards—she'd taken the precaution of wearing an ordinary pair of pink nylon panties under the ruffled white lace ones that came with the dress in order that too much of her wouldn't be visible when she sat down. Her stockings were glittering metallic silver net, so bright they cast reflections, and her shoes were silver, too. Her makeup, applied by Dhahaba, was absolutely perfect. She had a bouquet of golden-brown speckled orchids in her hands.

When she reached his side, Harry could feel her trembling, so he whispered in precisely the right, light, mocking tone,

"You're too gorgeous to be for real, Miss Anne!"

"But I am for real, Harry," she whispered back. "To-day, anyhow . . ."

Then the ceremony began.

Monsieur le Maire made a speech.

"Never have I been more proud," he said, "to be a citizen of *la Belle* France, with her traditions of *liberté, égalité, et fraternité,* than I am today. To see before me *ces deux beaux et charmants enfants* of different races who in their own country would not be allowed to sit in the same classroom, but *ici, chez nous,* can freely join together their hearts, their fortunes, and their lives, is *très émouvant.* I am happy to assist at this wedding. I pray that it will mark the beginning of a new era *chez notre grands amis, Les Etats Unis,* who are so advanced in things material and, it is sad to relate, so backward in things of the spirit . . .

"*Mes enfants*, love one another, honor and cherish the *amour* that today publicly you pledge. And now—"

Mister the Mayor looked around that dingy courtroom and intoned, solemnly, the French equivalent of:

"If there be any person present who knows of a valid reason why this man and this woman should not be joined in the bonds of Holy Wedlock, let him speak now, or forever henceforth hold his peace!"

From the doorway that dry, sibilant, mocking voice said in a stage whisper more penetrating than a shout—

"*Moi!*"

Harry heard Kathy's sharp intake of breath; Ouija's gasp; Buzz Merlin's "Hot damn!"; Fats Winkler's groaning, "Now that really tears the rag right off the bush!" before he turned and saw Raoul Levi lounging against the doorframe, still clad in his filthy blue jeans, his equally filthy turtleneck sweater, and with the same—if anything, filthier—bloodcaked bandage wrapped around his head.

"*Jeune homme!*" the mayor said. "This is not the place for jesting!"

"But I do not jest, your Honor," Raoul said. "I object to this wedding as unnecessary. Marriage is a decadent bourgeois institution which should be abolished. Let 'Arry and Kathy go away and love another as free men and women should, unbound by contracts and empty legalisms—held together only by that love, in perfect liberty to part once that love has ceased. That, your Honor, would be the civilized way of doing things—"

The mayor drew himself up to his full height and thundered:

"And their children, what of them, *mon jeune en-ragé?*"

Raoul smiled.

"Oh, let them all be bastards, got with whatever varying partners strike their individual fancy, as well as with each other, and reared at the charge of the state!" he said.

"Police!" the mayor shrieked. "Police! Take him! Arrest him! Throw him into—"

"No, your Honor, if you please," Harry said gently. "He is a friend of mine, and he has been, as you can see, badly injured. I think his condition is in part responsible for his words. Besides, he will not interrupt the ceremony further. Will you, Raoul?"

"If you ask me not to, *mon vieux*—and if your Kathy promises me a kiss," Raoul said.

"Done," Harry said.

"Very well, your Honor, I withdraw my objections," Raoul said solemnly. "Let this *carnaval* proceed!"

The mayor got through the rest of it, though it was obvious that he was badly shaken.

"I now pronounce you man and wife!" he said at last, like a drill sergeant. "Have the goodness to kiss *votre épousée, jeune mari!*"

Harry bent then and touched her lips with his own for one brief instant; but, when he tried to draw back, Kathy put her right hand behind his head, and with her left, sight unseen, tossed her bouquet directly at Ouija, who caught it deftly enough. Then Kathy brought her left hand up and locked it about his neck, and, going up on tiptoe, clung her mouth to his through a slow, soft, unbearable stretching of the stuff of time that abruptly walled out sound, so that he didn't even hear Ouija's outraged gasp, Fats' prayerful moan, the rasp of Ahmad's "Ya Allah!" or the nervous titter of the black girls' laughter.

He felt the afternoon sun on his closed eyelids as heat, as a burning, sensed it through them as a reddish purple; and his nostrils were filled with her various fragrances: a perfume by Worth of Paris called, oddly, Je Reviens, a lingering hint of bath soap, a kind of deodorant, and beneath it all—faint, elusive—what must have been her, striking through all that chemical armor under the whiplash of the mindless little glands that effortlessly deny the mind's dominance, or end it. He could feel her against him so weightless, soft, insubstantial that the arhythmic halt and flutter and racing beat of her heart were more vivid than the crush of cloth, the cling of flesh. Her mouth was a sweet sighing, warm moist taste of lipstick, a brief, exploratory hot thrusting of tongue tip, that ended at once in a gasp of what must have been recognition, or even shame. Then her lips went cold suddenly, turned icy, salt-tasting, quivering, so that the spell was broken, the magic gone, and he pushed her a little away from him.

He looked down at her, seeing the tears streaking her makeup, turning her eyes into mirrors of glazed, unfocused anguish that reflected only the curiously distorted image of his black face.

"What did *that* mean, Kathy?" he asked her.

"Don't know. That I'm crazy, probably. Insane. No—stark, raving mad," Kathy said.

Chapter Nine

"No," Harry said quietly, "that's enough, Kathy—"

Kathy looked at him. Then she put the champagne glass back on the table, untasted.

"You're perfectly right, darling," she said.

"And cut that out, too, that 'darling' business," Harry said grimly. "This is where the put on stops, Miss Anne."

She looked away from him across Ahmad's lawn towards where Fats Winkler was shoveling canapés into his mouth with both hands. Then she looked back at Harry. Her eyes were a little moist, but her control was superb.

"No, Harry, this isn't where it stops," she said. "Not yet. It stops later on. Tonight, in fact."

That, Harry thought with reluctant admiration, is one hell of a phrase. A statement that can mean either one of two things as opposite as day and night. Or, as living and dying. But don't you worry your sweet little addled head over it none a'tall, girl baby. Going to make it easy for you. Drive straight through to Nice. Go by that flossy fleabag so fast that—

"Harry—" Kathy said, "they—they're bringing your instruments! The servants, I mean. Are you—you and the band—going to play?"

"Yes, baby," Harry said.

"But why, Harry? This is our wedding reception. You don't have to entertain people. Not today, anyhow. It doesn't seem—"

"Right. But it is, Miss Anne. Item one, it's not entertainment, it's a wedding gift. And it's not for people—it's for one Kathy Temporarily Forbes, née Nichols. So just you sit tight and listen, baby. Listen good!"

Then he was gone, limping away from her across the crisp perfection of Ahmad's lawn before she could think of anything to say at all.

When she heard those first few mocking bars of "Dixie," Kathy's mouth tightened in real anger; but when the new theme emerged, her anger died. That theme was so playful, so gay. It was filled with sunlight, laughter, with a sort of musical gibberish that sounded like a little girl talking to a puppy dog, or a kitten, maybe. She listened with delight as the row of clockwork dolls click-clacked in, and to the march of the teddy bears. She wasn't even aware that both Dhahaba and Ouija were moving towards her, driven by feminine curiosity, studying her face.

But when that second, darker theme started spiraling around the sunny beat, choking it, strangling it, making the music go atonal, cacophonic, harsh, strident even with confusion, with doubt, she caught her breath. She let it out slowly when Harry blew one high, clear, soaring note that was like a shaft of sunlight lancing through storm clouds; but, by the time she heard that feverish, syncopated beat, shrill with hysterical laughter, glasses clinking, the sultry, slow, pounding note of sensuality with its grinding, pelvic, hip-writhing rhythm, so physical that it came over like the smell of sweat, striking through perfume, like the hot, salt taste of blood from a savagely bitten lip, she was already crying, although she didn't even know she was.

Dhahaba was beside her now, looking at her with both pity and concern; but Ouija stopped a meter away, and stared into Kathy's face with an expression that combined slow dawning recognition, gloating triumph, and absolutely feral hatred at one and the same time. Which, as Harry would have said, was quite a trick, but little Ouija managed it.

But, to Kathy, they weren't there, didn't exist. There was nothing in the world but that string of whimpering, half-hearted "No's" that Harry was blowing now; that cruelly literal description of a girl child's facing, for the first time in her life, the fact of being female as opposed to merely feminine; that she is a she-thing, bitch-thing, panting, wild, so that that last high, throat-tearing, screamed out "No!" was directed more at herself, was far more the hurt, sick, astonished protest of a delicate mind at the appalling treachery that the body it inhabited, and was supposed to control, was capable of; at her own will-less, degrading, more than half-masochistic surrender, than any serious attempt to stop what all too obviously was going on.

Quite suddenly, she had to sit down. Somebody, Dhahaba, probably, pushed a chair under her; and she sat there, listening to Harry's clarinet singing her blues, that gut-deep wail of utter desolation, self-loathing, anguished hurt. The sickness that rose in her then was swamp-slime green, and she was desperately afraid she was going to faint, so she put her head down between her knees—hearing from very far off, from another country, the clarinet's groping strain: that seeking for *le temps* which, despite Proust, can never be *retrouvé*, searching for innocence irretrievably lost, for sunlight, laughter, joy all gone—until the house, the garden, Harry, the band, Ahmad, his family, the guests, and the servants stopped their maypole dance, all the more revolting for being so insanely slow and stately, about the exact spot occupied by her bright head.

She had mastered herself—shaking off Dhahaba's hand from her shoulder, saying angrily, "Oh, *laissez-moi, je vous prie! Je suis tout à fait bien!*"—had recovered, was sitting upright in the chair when Harry blew that last, long slow dying line of acceptance, resignation, defeat; but, hearing the echoing silence following that *andante molte lento*, that *dolce fa niente* description of what maturity actually is, feeling it, she did exactly what the girl in the *boîte* had done the first time Harry had played "Little Girl Lost"—that is, with a gesture that was pure, abject recognition, she buried her face in her hands and cried.

Ahmad, of course, had already started towards her at a loping run the moment she'd been overcome with giddiness and doubled over with her head down between her knees. But before he was near enough to say or do anything, Dhahaba put her arms around Kathy's quivering shoulders and whispered with real pity, "Ah, *non, ma pauvre petite!* You must not cry!" A moment later, Ahmad got there and bent toward her, saying worriedly: "What is the matter little Kathy? Are you ill?"

And it was only then that Ouija said it, calmly, clearly, contemptuously, not even loud:

"*Malade*, Papa? *Peut-être.* You could call it that. But it is an illness of her own making. Cannot you see that she is *enceinte, cette petite putain-là?* And that *son bâtard* is not of Harry, *j'en suis certaine, moi.*"

Kathy straightened up at once, stared at Ouija. Then with that absolute mastery of self that was her finest quality, she said:

"Why don't you ask Harry that, Ouija? That is—if you dare!"

Ouija whirled then, faced Harry, who had come limping towards them—who, by then, was nearly there, his eyes bleak with pain, with worry. She was laughing, but her laughter was mirthless, scornful, more anguished than crying would have been.

"*Si j'ose!*" she said. "How little she knows me, *ta respectueuse!* Tell me: Is it yours, this child, 'Arree? Is it? *Je te demande la vérité! C'est à toi, son bébé?*"

Harry's face was gray with weariness, but his voice, when he spoke, was gentle.

"If there is a baby, which is a thing that you, Ouija, do not, nor cannot know, it is mine. In all ways, and absolutely."

Then he came on, limping heavily to where Kathy sat in the garden chair. Stood there looking at her.

"I wrote that for you, baby. A true thing for a little girl lost, because what I feel for her is true. Only I forgot one thing, didn't I?"

"What thing, Harry?" Kathy said. The words came out muffled, humid with choked-back tears.

"That the truth hurts too goddamned bad. Guess I got carried away. And, anyhow, you're still one up on me, Kathy—"

"One up on you?" Kathy said, her voice uncomprehending, slow.

"Yes," Harry said bleakly, " 'cause losing you is going to hurt me worse."

Then he half turned to walk away from there; but Kathy came up out of the chair and caught him by the arm.

"Take me away from here, Harry! Right now!" she said.

"Where're we going to stop, Harry?" Kathy said. "To-night, I mean? It—it's getting awfully late now, and—"

Harry didn't look at her. He set the Farcel Vega up into a beautiful four-wheel drift at an even one hundred and forty-five kilometers an hour, bending Ahmad's bolide around a long, long sweeping curve as expertly as a racing driver.

"We don't," he said. "We drive straight through."

"But—but—" Kathy said, "didn't Ahmad—"

"Reserve the bridal suite for us at the Hotel de Paris et de la Poste in Sens-les-Bains? He did. But there's a plane out of Nice for New York at eight-forty-five to-morrow morning. With any luck, you can be on it."

"Oh," Kathy said. Then, "You're *that* anxious to be rid of me, Harry?"

He glanced at her, his black face still, unsmiling; looked back at the road, and said,

"When I was in the base hospital at Saigon, and even later on, when they flew me to the big one in Japan, I learned one thing—"

"What thing, Harry?" Kathy whispered.

"What my limits were. The precise point where I started screaming my guts out. So now I quit while I'm still ahead—"

"Oh," Kathy said. Then, "Is that Sens down there?"

"Yes," Harry said.

"Do we—do we pass by the hotel? I'd like to—to see it, anyhow. One more thing to remember, Harry . . ."

"Have to. It's on the main street. And Nationale Cinq goes right through Sens. You'll see it all right. It's just beyond the cathedral . . ."

She didn't say anything else, until they were creeping by the cathedral, caught in a long line of trucks. That was before the strikes, and gasoline was still plentiful. Then she whispered:

"Harry—I—I'm so tired. Couldn't we—"

"No," Harry said.

So he was entirely unprepared. They were directly in front of the hotel, a low, yellow structure with a red roof, which boasts one of the finest chefs in all France, when she did it. Her hand shot out, closed over the ignition key, twisted it, jerked it out of the contact-lock.

The big Chrysler engine in the Farcel Vega coughed just once, then died.

"Kathy, for the love of Christ!" Harry began. But, before he could move or think or do anything to stop her, she'd already pulled the front of her blouse out and was busily pushing the key down the front of her brassiere, between her breasts.

He sat there, staring at her, and trembling a little.

"Mind telling me *why* you did that, Miss Anne?" he said.

"For that. To stop you from calling me 'Miss Anne' in that tone of voice, now, henceforth, and forevermore. And—and—because—"

"Because what?" Harry said.

"Because—a man's entitled to—to his wedding night," Kathy whispered. "And—and so am I, damnit! Now come on!"

That next morning, when Harry stopped the car in front of La Pyramide in the little town of Vienne, fourteen kilometers south of Lyon, she still had both her arms wrapped around his right bicep, and her bright, tousled head resting against his shoulder. She hadn't moved from that position since they'd left Sens at 9:45 A.M., which had made driving a tricky *grand tourisme* like the Farcel Vega something of a chore. So far as he'd been able to see from the occasional glance he'd thrown in her direction—the traffic on Nationale Sept having been as murderous as usual—she'd kept her eyes closed tight the whole time. Certainly she hadn't spoken one single word. And yet he was sure she hadn't slept. But now, as he cut the ignition, he saw the sudden, startled flash of greenish blue.

"Why are we stopping, Harry?" she said.

"To eat. Have to, you know. This joint's pretty good. In fact, it's the best . . ."

"Oh, Harry," she wailed, "I couldn't eat. I simply couldn't!"

"Girl baby, you've got to. For both of you, you know . . ."

"For both of us?" she whispered. Then she got it. So she said, "Ohhhhh God!" bent her head, and cried.

He stared at her. He'd seen her cry many times before; but never like this. She cried aloud, shamelessly. Her whole small, fragile body shook. The sobs grated from her throat as though the very tissues of it were tearing, alternating with a moaning sound that shuddered all the way up from her solar plexus, shredding gut and nerve and lungs as it came. The way she cried now was absolutely, unspeakably awful. He couldn't listen to it. It wasn't to be borne.

"Kathy—" he said, reproachfully.

She whirled upon him, her small hands doubled into fists. She pounded his chest with both of them, as hard as she could.

"Did you have to remind me, Harry?" she raged. "Did you?"

He caught her wrists, held them.

"Kathy, please!" he said.

"Wasn't—last night—enough for you?" she got out. "How many times do you have to—to break my heart?"

"Sorry, baby," he said.

"My little bastard. The little son of a creep you're giving your name to. I hate him! I hate him, Harry! I wish he were dead!"

"Don't say that, Kathy," Harry said wearily. "Exercise some more of that Anglo-Saxon sense of fair play that drove you into my bed last night—like a nice grit-your-teeth-and-bear-it little lamb. It's not the kid's fault."

She stared at him.

"You—you're right," she whispered. "As usual. I—I don't hate him. I hate *me*. I wish *I* were dead!"

"Why do you wish that, Kathy?" he said.

"I *am* in a way," she said. "You've done what you set out to do, Harry. You've destroyed me."

"So," he said, and his voice was gray suddenly, toneless. "I was wondering how you were going to do it—"

Her eyes gave a little, startled leap; then, very slowly, they penciled his face with reflected light, discerning it now, perceiving it, which was a new thing for her, who—at least as far as the darker, alien breeds were concerned—had always been content before with the slightly blank, unfocused gaze that either doesn't see at all, or sees only what it wants to see.

"How I was going to do what, Harry?" she said.

"Arrange—last night—to suit your preconceived notions. Little Kathy, playing fair. Being noble. Recompensing this poor child of sin and sorrow for his efforts on her behalf—in her own peculiar fashion. The sweet, sacrificial lamb—shutting her eyes tight and thinking of —the playing fields of Durham, Nawth Ca'lina, shall we say, Miss Anne? That would have been acceptable, wouldn't it? Only I kind of, sort of, dented that one for you a little, didn't I? So now, this. The oldest one in the books: the big black burly brute who—destroyed you. That *was* the way you put it, wasn't it, Miss Anne?"

She stared at him, and her mouth made a soft, pink O of utter astonishment.

"Oh, no!" she said. "Oh, no, Harry! You—you've got it all wrong!"

"*I've* got it wrong?" he said. "Me?"

"Yes, *you*. 'Cause I—I'm back from that long, bad trip, remember? I don't lie to myself anymore. I wish I could. About last night. Oh God *how* I wish I could!"

Harry looked at her. But he didn't say anything, because he couldn't think of a single word that would make sense under the present circumstances.

"So, destroyed," Kathy said. "Smashed. Shattered. Pick your own word, Mister Lover Man! You did it. Only it wasn't—physical. You weren't that crude. I wish you had been. It would have been—better—"

"Better?" Harry said.

"Yes, yes—better! Then maybe I *could* do what you thought I *was* doing—pretending to myself that you—that you—brutalized me last night. That—the animal—at the festivities—that unspeakable little panting bitch—wasn't me!"

"Kathy—" he said, sorrowfully.

"Only I can't. You want some more of this down home, country-revival-meeting confession? All right, lover, here it is! I'll admit I was fully prepared to—to be roughed up a little, even hurt—oh, all right, all right! Those stereotypes again! And I wasn't—except—"

"Except what?" Harry said.

"Except that—that much—pleasure—is a kind of pain."

"So?" Harry whispered.

"So—destroyed. You're looking at a corpse, Harry. Unmarked. No scars on it. No visible wounds. But dead, all the same. It was—pleasured to death last night. Delighted into extinction. No. That's not right. Not quite, anyhow."

"Lord!" Harry said. "Then what *is* right, Kathy?"

"I'm not going to tell you," she said. "You know too goddamned much about women, now. So, Mister Expert at—at what? Let me think. At—at the annihilation-of-personality-through-ecstasy, shall we call it? Yes, let's do call it that! You've done it. You've destroyed me. *Me*, Kathy Nichols. Not my only-too-responsive body—reduced—no, not reduced! Exalted. Exalted into—into what, Harry? You tell me. I don't know."

"Womanhood," Harry said. "All right?"

"All right. I'll buy that. Into womanhood. For the first time, damnit! So you didn't kill—my body. Not this hateful, brainless little apparatus of flesh, happily grinding out one exquisitely crippling spasm after another, as though it were trying to discover just how close—pleasure —can get to pure, screaming agony—without the results being—fatal, say . . ."

"Kathy," Harry said sorrowfully, "you mustn't torment yourself like this. You mustn't. Not only is it sick, but—"

But she went on as though she hadn't heard him. As she hadn't, really. She was listening to her own thought processes, or perhaps to her fast-beating heart.

"I thought of that. Of dying, I mean. Only my body let me down. My treacherous bitch kitty of a body that wasn't even decent enough—or was too blamed starved, more likely!—to take that way out. And that possibility existed, Harry! I even got close to it! I concentrated on that, I mean on converting our—let me go on calling it lovemaking, will you, huh, please? I'm still too inhibited to say the ugly, honest word—into the damn' finest suicide technique in human history . . ."

"Lord!" Harry said.

"So—my death—wasn't physical. But, all the same,

you murdered me. The real me. My conception of myself. Who I am—or rather who I thought I was. That was what you were trying to do all along, wasn't it?"

"No," Harry said. "Not *you*, baby. Just—Miss Anne."

"Oh!" she said and stared at him.

"Have I?" he said.

She sat there, her gaze turned inward, contemplating what most people can't bear to, ever: herself. What she was. What she had to be.

"Yes," she said. "God, yes!"

"So now what?" Harry teased, consciously trying to break the tension, divert her from her morbid chain of thought. "Do I get let off easy? Or do you call out the Bedsheet Boys? String my black carcass up so high that even the buzzards would need an oxygen mask to reach me?"

"No," she said, grimly, "but I ought to. Punish you, somehow, I mean. I grant you that *she*, Miss Anne, wasn't fit to live. But the *way* you demolished her—us— was very nearly unforgivable, Harry. Wait! I don't think you understand. Not yet. I—I have to get there, slowly. I—I could have borne your being so—so goddamned expert—after all, you have been married, and you must have had a million women by now—"

"A million, baby? Good Lord!"

"Enough, anyhow. To—to have learned, *everything*. To you, a girl's only another kind of musical instrument, isn't she? To play—touching all the right keys—oh, ever so gently!—until she sounds all the notes you want. Coming downstairs this morning was *the* most awful thing I ever had to endure in my whole life! They were all looking at me and grinning, Harry! 'Cause—'cause they heard me! Everybody in the hotel did! And—and

the bishop in the cathedral! And the mayor in *la mairie!*
And—"

"Now, baby," Harry said, "you weren't *that* noisy."

"I was, and you know it. Doesn't matter, now. It's
not even the main point."

"Then what is the main point?" Harry said.

"Something I'm—I'm afraid to ask you," Kathy said.
"You always tell the truth—I know that. Only this time,
I maybe couldn't stand it. The truth, I mean."

Harry stared at her.

"Besides, it doesn't matter. 'Cause maybe she and I
were twins, anyhow. Siamese twins, with only one heart
between us. So maybe to kill her—Miss Anne—you had
to kill me, too. Anyhow, that's what it feels like. Only—"

"Only?" Harry said.

She faced him then, her eyes blind, scalded.

"Was I—sexed to death—or *loved* a little, Harry? Was
any—of that terrible tenderness—for *me?* Or was it all
what I've been clawing my own insides bloody-raw
thinking this morning? When you set out to—to chastise
me—*that* way, didn't it—the tenderness, I mean, sort of
float up from your subconscious? Wasn't it a—a condi-
tioned reflex, doled out to me, secondhand? Learned
from *her*—from Fleur!"

"Baby—" Harry said.

"Were we alone last night? Or wasn't—her ghost—
between us in that bed? That's what I thought—this
morning, when my mind came back, and I could think
again. You ride, so you know what has to be done to a
badly crippled horse. I'm that hurt now, Harry—or
worse. So—give it to me, right between the eyes—or save
me. No, you *can't* save me. I'm dead either way. Only,
in that one sense, it would be more acceptable . . ."

Harry looked at her.

"*If* I follow you, and I'm not sure I do," he said gently, "I have only to tell you what I've been eating my own guts out over all morning—"

"And that is?" Kathy whispered.

"Last night, for the first time since I met her—I forgot Fleur. Forgot her completely. I'm ashamed of that, but there it is—"

"Oh, Harry!" she said, and kissed him.

"Have I—saved you, then?" he said.

"No. You can't. You never could. I don't exist. But you've given—Kathy Nichols, anyhow—a better reason for being dead."

Harry put out his index finger and poked the tip of her nose with it, playfully, tenderly.

"Then who's this?" he said.

She put her arms around his neck. Looked him straight in the face.

"Kathy Forbes. Forever. As long as there's breath in me. And—hunger—and hurting. And so, because that—can't be—I'm dead."

"Don't see why the hell it can't," Harry said.

"Item one, I'm white. Item two, you're black. Item three, if I may quote your dearest darling Ouija, '*Elle est enceinte, cette petite putain-là!*' Meaning me. She's right. On both counts, lover. I definitely am pregnant. And I'm a whore, too—at least at heart. Proved that last night, didn't I?"

"Stop it!" Harry said. "You can't live your life on Ouija's terms, Kathy. And other people's stupid prejudices haven't a goddamned thing to do with you and me—"

"Oh yes, they do. Life is all prejudice, Harry. Including yours. And they're the ones we've got to look at now. 'Cause mine are gone. I buried 'em in the grave with Miss Anne. So, yours. The one's you've got. That you have to have if you're really a man, and if you—love me —even the teeniest little bit. Could you—stand—seeing every day—my little Creep? My little, all-white, half-French, bastard Creep, and being reminded that your—wife—that your wife—"

"Was once a sweet, lame-brained innocent who didn't know any better? Yes. Why yes, of course."

"I was going to say, was once 'an easy lay.' But let it go. Thank you for putting it—so gently, Harry. But then, you're nearly always gentle, aren't you? Gentle—and—and sweet. So goddamned sweet! That's why I won't let you—even try this. Why I won't inflict the little Creep on you. Why I condemn myself to—to loneliness. All the rest of my life."

He was beaten, then, and he knew it. By his own hesitation; by his aching doubt. Could I stand it? he thought. Could I? He said:

"The rest of your life's a long time, Kathy. You'll—"

"No, I won't! What's the use of—of taking up with a boy when I know I'll only compare him with you? And there's only *one* you, damnit. So, as I said before—you've killed me, Harry. Or blinded me, anyhow. So I can't *see* anybody else. Nobody, Harry . . ."

"Lord!" Harry said.

She grinned at him suddenly, made an impish face.

"Except—maybe—somebody who—who isn't white," she said. " 'Cause now and then I'll look at a colored boy and—and sort of wonder—"

"Honey," Harry said, "you just promoted me. From here on in, I'm the Grand Imperial Wizard of the Ku

Klux Klan. Now come on, damnit! You've simply got
to eat—"

He thought, that's it: Joke. Play Pagliacci in blackface.
Cool it, brother. Don't even stand too close to her, else
she might hear how your guts are screaming . . .

He took her by the arm, and led her into La Pyramide.

She did eat, after all, with quite surprising appetite.
Of course, the food at La Pyramide would tempt an
anchorite saint into gluttony, Harry conceded. What's
more, she downed two or three glasses of Châteauneuf
du Pape over and above the quantity that was strictly
good for her. But under those peculiarly bittersweet circumstances, he hadn't the heart to stop her.

When he had cheerfully paid the astronomical *addition*, reflecting that, after all, great art, which is what
the cooking at La Pyramide truly is, is actually priceless,
he turned to her.

"Come on, baby—" he said.

But she shook her head, grinned at him, and said,
"No."

"But, Kathy, you can't just sit there—"

"Oh, yes, I can. At least until you promise to find a
nice quiet hotel room right here in this town. Where I
can go to bed with you. Again. All the rest of today. And
tonight. Tomorrow, we can go on to Nice. After all,
Papa did give me two weeks—"

"I," Harry said bleakly, "would give you more than
that, Kathy. I'd give you all the rest of my life."

She bent her head, looked up again.

"And I—I'd give you mine—if it weren't for the little
Creep . . ."

"Don't call him that," Harry said. "He's going to be

a beautiful baby. He has to be—being yours. And any-how—" his voice took on a note of urgency, as painful for her to listen to as her crying had been for him— "I'd never even remember how he got started. I'd love the little bastard as though he were my own, because, after all, if it hadn't been for him, I'd never even have known you—"

"Oh, Harry!" Kathy wailed, and got up from there. "Don't talk! Don't talk anymore, please! Just take me somewhere and—love me. 'Til I can't move. 'Til I'm all —hollow—and floating—and so damned relaxed that—"

"You feel incorporeal, ethereal, and sublime," Harry said. "The way you really are, anyhow . . ."

She stared at him.

"Lord!" she said, imitating his own tone of mock admiration. "Will you please, please, please, please quit talking and come on?"

Chapter
Ten

Which was why they didn't get to Nice until the morning of May 18, the same day that General Charles de Gaulle inclined his proud and stubborn head slightly in the direction of fate and came back from Roumania twenty-four hours ahead of schedule. They checked into the Negresco—because, as Harry discovered to his disgust, the fine old Ruhl had closed its august doors two years before for the simple reason that it was losing more money than even the government could afford. Having changed, bathed, and rested—or rather not rested, for the honestly intended repose turned into an hour's hungry and desperate lovemaking which ended with Kathy weeping in Harry's arms—they went out and walked up the Promenade des Anglais until they came to Cooks Wagon Lits.

It was a madhouse, as was every other travel agency in France by then. Would-be travelers were screaming at the clerks in a dozen languages. One enraged Englishman shook his fist in the manager's face. Through all the roarings, the shouts, the clerks repeated over and over again like weary robots:

"*Plus de vols, M'sieu. Non, aucune ligne airienne ne les a. Grève générale.* No, sir, no flights at all. General strike. *Oui, je sais, je sais! Il vous faut absolument rentrer chez vous. Mais, Madame, qu'est ce que vous voulez que je fasse? Ce n'est pas de toute ma faute à moi, ce grève! Les lignes étrangères? Elles aussi*—Yes, sir, the foreign lines too. What's that? Of course they haven't struck! But how can they land when the radio operators, the control-tower men, the drivers of the gasoline trucks, the —*Es tut mir leid, mein Herr, aber ich kann nichts dafür* —*Lo siento muchísimo, Señores, pero todos los vuelos son cancelados. Huelga general, entendido? Vous dites? La révolution? Quelle révolution? Vous blaguez, non?*"

"What is it, then," Harry said politely, "that one does?"

"*Vous avez une voiture, M'sieu?*" the clerk said.

"Yes, we have a car," Harry said.

"*Et aussi quelque litres d'essence?*"

"That also. I filled the tank at Cagnes-sur-Mer."

"*Vous avez eu de la chance,*" the clerk said.

"Luck?" Kathy said. "What do you mean, M'sieu?"

"I mean," the clerk said, "that now you and *votre*—husband—can drive the sixty-nine kilometers to the *frontière de l'Italie. Là bas,* there is not the problem. *Les Italiens, eux,* have plenty of *essence,* since the chauffeurs of their *cisterns-camions* have not struck, there being no general strike in Italy. You cross the *frontière.* From San Remo, you take the *autostrada* to Turin. From Turin, you drive to Domodossola, then over the Simplon Pass into *la belle Suisse.* You cross that *tout petit et si ennuyant* country to *Genève. A Genève il y a des avions pour* New York. *Ou, si vous preferiez, vous pouvez aller à* Rome. At Rome there are also flights to *Les Etats-Unis.* Simple, is it not so?"

"Very," Harry said. "Thank you infinitely. C'mon, Kathy baby, let's get out of here . . ."

"Harry—" Kathy said sadly, once they were in the car, "I—I guess I *had* better go—home, hadn't I?"

"Yes, baby," Harry said.

"Ohhhhh, Harry!" Kathy said, and hid her face against his neck.

"Sorry, girl baby," Harry said.

"*You're* sorry!" Kathy said. "Harry—if—if I find some way to—to come back—will you—will you wait for me?"

"Don't talk nonsense, Kathy," Harry said.

"Right," she said bitterly. "It is nonsense, isn't it?"

"Yes," Harry said.

"Ouija," Kathy said. "She caught my bouquet without half trying. As—as easily—as she's going to—to catch *you,* damn her! On the rebound, while I—"

"While you'll have all the Robert E. Rebs lined up in queues. Panting," Harry said.

"Harry—" Kathy said. "Let's stop this. Please."

"All right," Harry said. "Consider it stopped."

"Good. Where're we going now?"

"To the hotel. To get your things. Then to Italy," Harry said. "After that, Switzerland. Geneva."

"Oh, no!" Kathy said.

"Oh, yes," Harry said.

They got to Geneva at midday, Monday the twentieth, only to find that every American tourist in France—except for those who had managed to get to Brussels or Luxembourg—had had the same idea. Or had been similarly advised. And, in both cases, with priority. The airport's waiting room looked like a refugee camp. Some of the tourists had *vin ordinaire* and sausages. They were sharing with one another. The atmosphere was gay. Most of them seemed to find the whole thing a lark.

But Harry and Kathy didn't. They sat in the waiting room and waited. From time to time, Harry made the rounds of the ticket counters of the various airlines. No luck. No seats. *Complet.*

"Oh, Harry!" Kathy said suddenly, "you forgot!"

"I forgot what?" Harry said.

"To—to send me that telegram! To the wedding reception! So you could show it to them afterwards and—"

"*Merde!*" Harry said. Then, "What difference does it make now, baby?"

"None," Kathy said. "I—I hope that if I do get on a plane that it—that it crashes! Splatters me and the little Creep all over—"

Harry clamped his hand over her mouth.

"Don't say that, Kathy!" he said. "Don't ever say a thing like that out loud!"

She looked at him.

"What would you do if it did?" she said.

"Cut my throat," Harry said.

"You would *not*," Kathy said. "You'll go back to Paris and let little Ouija—comfort you. In a horizontal position. Like I would right now if there were only a few less people around—"

"Kathy, baby, if you mention Ouija one more time, so help me, I'm going to belt you one!"

"Harry," Kathy said, "kiss me."

"Lord, baby—" Harry said.

"Please. That man over there. He's a Southerner. I can tell. Apart from the fact that he almost had a stroke when you put your hand over my mouth, it's written all over him. Let's see if we can't give him one. Apoplexy. Heart attack. The works."

Harry glanced across to the opposite bench. She was right. The man, about sixty, was beet red, and glowering.

"All right, baby," he said, and kissed her. A long time. So long they both forgot about the man.

When they looked up, he was gone.

"Couldn't take it, could you, Robert E.?" Harry said.

The hours wore on.

"Harry," Kathy said, "you—you'd better go back to Paris—and—and leave me here. 'Cause if this goes on too long and Papa flies over here and finds us together, he'd kill you."

"That would take some doing," Harry said. "Besides, who's going to tell him we're in Geneva?"

"Oh, he'd find out. Papa's smart—in all the wrong ways. Please, Harry—I—I'm scared—"

"No," Harry said.

"Turn me loose, lover," Kathy said.

"No," Harry said again.

"Please. I have to go to the little girls' room. While I'm gone, buy me a sandwich and a Coke, will you? I know it's awfully unromantic, but—but I'm so hungry I'm half fainting!"

"Why, damnit, so am I!" Harry said with real wonder. "All right, Kathy . . ."

As at most airports, the rest rooms in the one at Geneva are downstairs on the lower level. Kathy disappeared down the escalator, and Harry went to the lunch counter. He got back to the place where they were sitting before she did. In fact, she was so long in returning that he was beginning to worry, to fear that in her delicate state she had passed out downstairs in the ladies' room, when he saw her coming up the stairs.

But the feeling of relief, of tenderness that flooded over him at the sight of her small, fragile figure vanished as soon as she was close. She didn't so much as look at the sandwich and the Coca Cola he held out to her. Her face was ghost-white. She was shaking. She said, "Oh, Harry, Harry!" And began to cry.

"Now, Kathy—" Harry said.

"Harry, that man! That Southerner! He—"

"By God," Harry said, "if he so much as said one nasty word to you, I'll—"

"No. He wasn't—nasty. Not really. Sort of—polite, in fact. He—he was waiting for me when I came out of the ladies' room. He just stood there looking at me, then he said, 'You going back home alone, or that boy going with you?' "

"What did you say to that?" Harry said.

"I said, 'What boy? I don't see any boys around here.' "

"And he?" Harry said.

" 'That colored fellow you're with. He going with you?' Then I said, 'You mean my husband? Unfortunately, no. He works in Paris . . .' "

"Then?" Harry said.

" 'Your folks know?' he said. And I said, 'I fail to see what business that is of yours, Mister.' Then he said, 'They don't. They can't. You're Southern. Can tell by your accent. So it *is* my business, or I'm making it mine, just like I hope your Pa would make it his if he caught *my* daughter doing what you are, honey.' So I said to him, 'There's mighty little you can do about it, Mister!' "

"What did he say then?" Harry whispered.

" 'There's a right smart bit I can do, honey—like for instance getting home some other way. Boat, maybe. Here, you take this, and don't argue. And don't you come back, honey. What you're doing is mighty wrong . . . the good Lord never intended for the races to mix. You hear me, child?' "

"And?" Harry said.

"He went out of the downstairs door with his luggage in his hands. Said to me, 'Bye now, honey. You do like I told you, you hear?' I—I didn't even answer him. He was getting into a taxi with his bags—and I—I stood there—and—and let him drive off—before I even thought to look—at—at what he'd put in my hand . . ."

"What was it?" Harry said, bleakly. But he already knew.

"This—" Kathy said, and held it out to him.

It was a first-class ticket on TWA Flight 206. And then, at that precise moment, as if to prove that hope is a jokesmith, a mocker, and a clown, the loudspeakers of the public-address system started their nasal rattle:

"*Messieurs les Passagèrs pour le Tay-Double-Uvay Vol deux-cent-six, déstination New-York, sont priés de se présenter à la porte numéro trois—départ immédiat . . .*"

"Dear God!" Kathy said.

Harry bent and kissed her mouth. It was cold and wet and salt with tears, some of which were his own.

"Bye, bye, girl baby," he said. Then he turned and left her standing there. While he still could.

Chapter Eleven

"Did you—" Otis Hatfield said.

"Go to his pad? Yes," Fats said. "Every mother-loving day since I found the car parked outside of this joint. Some days twice. Yesterday, three times. He ain't there. Bed ain't even mussed up."

"That little gray bitch!" Buzz Merlin said.

"Now, Buzz," Fats said, "we don't know—"

"Shit," Buzz said.

"Damn' if I dig it though," Otis said. "The way she

was swabbing his tonsils for him at the ceremony, a body'd think—"

"About grays, I don't think," Buzz said. "Mr. Charley's daughters, ain't they? Strictly four-F from where I sit: Feed 'em, feel 'em up, fuck 'em and forget 'em, says I. But Harry's a Southern boy. Been brainwashed, just like I said."

"Buzz—" Otis said, "don't hand me that crap. Little Kathy was mighty fine, and you know it. Way you was eyeing her at the wedding—"

"So what? So she's really stacked and has got a way of walking that makes a fellow get a hard on just watching her float by. Fine, Brother Otis! Great. For one night. A weekend. But I'll be shot with shit and get myself arrested for stinking if I'd buy the package permanent. You remember that hometown boy who was over here last year? First cat I ever met what made sense. 'Integration?' he used to say. 'Now don't that just grab you, Buzz? A chance to be with Mr. Charley, Miss Anne, and old Papa Rightoff—you know, right-off-that-hoss-and-onto-your-black-ass before you can get that "Yassuh!" out—all day long? Hell, man, I see more of Whitey than I *want* to, now. What I want is *more* segregation, not less. Only *I* want to do the segregating. When I get my cats trained good—and some of 'em is pretty fair shots now—we're gonna take over Georgia, Alabama, and Mississippi—and kick Mr. Charley, Miss Anne, and old Papa Rightoff the hell out. Our own vine and fig tree, Buzz. The Republic of Xania—where *black* is right, and white stay back!' "

"That," Fats sighed, "is exactly what the mule drops in the road, Buzz. Anyhow, I can't solve the race problem right now. Too worried about Harry. Romantic kind of a boy. Had to watch him every minute when lil' Fleur passed on. Look in his eyes I didn't like—"

"Fats," Otis said, "you don't think he'd—?"

"No," Fats said, "but I ain't sure enough in my mind not to worry. Who knows what any cat will do when the shit really hits the fan? Reckon I'll just get on my little red bicycle—"

"Jesus!" Buzz said, "if there ever was a sight, it's you on that kid's bike, Fats! Why didn't you get yourself one your size?"

"Couldn't," Fats said. "They was sold out. Everybody had the same idea. First time I rode over here on it, all them poor sorefooted folks who was walking to work 'cause there ain't a taxi, a bus, nor a metro working in this whole goddamn' miserable burg, clapped their hands and cheered. '*Regardez ce gros débrouillard!*' they says—and rushed off to buy themselves a *vélo*, too. Only there ain't none left. Bought the last bike in Paris. Anyhow, reckon I'd better have another look-see and—"

"Fats," Otis said, "was me, I wouldn't go over to the Left Bank tonight. Them kids is really got a mad on, now. Minister of the Interior announced they ain't gonna let that pretty lil' Jewboy come back—"

"Come back?" Buzz said. "Where's that redheaded lil' mother fucker gone?"

"Berlin," Otis said. "Exporting the revolution. Papers call him the traveling salesman of the Black Flag."

"The *Black* Flag?" Buzz said. "Don't tell me Danny the Red has gone and took up Negritude!"

"Naw," Fats said. "Black's for Anarchy, Red's for Mao, Trotsky, and Company. Not left enough for little Dan. Next to him, Raoul Levi's on the right side of Papa de Gaulle. You cats gonna sleep *here*?"

"Why not?" Buzz said. "With all the customers we've got these days? Hell, even the boss don't show up no more . . ."

"Ahmad? Spending all his time seeing that funky Raoul don't shove it up lil' Ouija," Otis said. "Now speaking of a classy piece of tail—"

"Jesus!" Fats said, "don't you characters *ever* think about anything else?"

"What else *is* there, Fats?" Buzz said.

"Oh, hell!" Fats began; but then he saw Jean Claude the waiter coming toward them. He was running.

"It is she!" he said. "*La petite épouse d'Arree! Au téléphone*—from New York! *Comme d'habitude, elle est hystérique*—especially when I told her he was not here. Now she wishes to speak with *you*, Fats . . ."

Fats looked at the others, a long, slow, sorrowing look. Then he said, "*D'accord*, Jean Claude, *je viens*."

"Fats!" Kathy's voice, over three thousand-odd miles of wire was faint, but perfectly clear. "Harry! Where is he? I want to talk to him! I've got to!"

"Sorry, girl baby," Fats said.

"Can't you find him?" Kathy wailed. "Can't you, Fats?"

"No. Told you he ain't here. Took a powder. Blew. Run out on us. Ain't nobody seen him in three days. Been to his pad. Bed hasn't even been slept in . . ."

"Oh, Fats!" Kathy said.

"Didn't know why, before. Now I do. So I got news for you, Kathy—you miserable lil' ball-whacking, man-ruining, no-good honky bitch. This is one scene you don't make no more. Not never. You stay on that side of the pond, girl friend. 'Cause if they find Harry floating in the Seine, like they're most likely going to, I'll see that you get yours. You read me, girl friend? You hear me talkin' to you?"

"Yes, Fats," Kathy said. Then, "Fats—he—he *sent* me away! I tried to stay! I tried—" Her voice drowned on her.

"Yes, girl baby?" Fats said. You softheaded, blind mother-gripper, he thought; but his tone was gentler, all the same.

"I've been sitting here in New York ever since. I haven't been home. I've missed eight airplanes, four trains, and Lord knows how many busses, 'cause—"

" 'Cause you love him, the put on's over, and you're for real. That's it, ain't it, baby girl?" Fats said. He believed her. He didn't know why he should have, but he did.

"Yes," Kathy said. "Fats, could you meet me? At Orly, I mean? 'Cause I'm going to be on the very next plane!"

Fats stood there. Then he sighed.

"Girl baby, there ain't no such animal," he said. "Planes, I mean. The general strike—"

"I know that! But I can get a flight to Brussels, and I'll charter an air taxi there! A light plane, Fats. There's no law saying a private plane can't come into France, is there? Is there, Fats?"

"No," Fats said, "so far as I know, anybody crazy enough to come here, can . . ."

"Then you'll meet me? Will you, Fats? I'll call you from Brussels. I'll let you know when to—"

Fats stared into the black mouthpiece of the telephone. Then he sighed again, very softly.

"Girl baby, you don't know what you're asking, but I'll sure Lord try," he said.

"*Non*, I regret, Mademoiselle, but I cannot," the air-taxi pilot said. "*Ça, c'est tout à fait impossible—*"

"*Pourquoi?*" Kathy said.

"First, Mademoiselle has *trop d'équipage*—too much luggage—and *mon oiseau est trop petit.* Look at him, *là bas. Un monomoteur.* A single-engine Jodel. He is a very brave little *avion* but he cannot lift so much baggage and also enough gasoline to arrive at Paris . . ."

"I'll leave my bags!" Kathy said. "I'll take only my overnight case. Put the rest in storage! I'll—"

"Wait, *gentille petite dame.* There are *encore des difficultés—mon coucou* can carry enough gasoline to get us to Orly, but not enough to get me back to *Bruxelles. Comme vous savez bien,* they have no gas *là bas.* And I have not the *envie* to remain in Paris. Even the *Folies-Bergères* is closed. Besides, they are mad, the French. At the moment, Paris is *beaucoup trop dangereux—*"

"Oh, no!" Kathy said.

"*Pauvre petite,*" the pilot said. "*Il vous faut absolument aller à Paris?*"

"Yes," Kathy said. "I absolutely must go to Paris!"

"*Attendez, donc. J'ai une idée . . .*"

"Where are you going?" Kathy said. "Please don't leave me. I—"

"*Attendez, ma belle.* We *Belges* have soft hearts. I go to look for *mon copain.* His bird is *plus gros.* A *bimoteur. Peut-être,* he'll—"

"Oh, please!" Kathy said.

The pilot came back with his friend. The friend was huge. He wore a fiery red beard. His face was red, too, but a different shade. A whiskey-red, Kathy thought.

He stared at Kathy. Closed one bright blue eye.

"*Vous avez vraiment de la chance*, Mademoiselle!" he said.

"Then you'll take me?" Kathy said. "You really will?"

"*Bien sûr.* But it is not in my taking you to Paris that your luck consists, my ravishing little blonde—"

"Then in what does it consist, *mon Capitaine?*" Kathy said.

"In that to fly a Piper Apache with reasonable safety, one must keep both hands on the controls!" the red-bearded pilot said.

"*Capitaine*—" Kathy said.

"Don't call me *Capitaine,*" Red Beard said. "Call me Willy. *C'est mon nom*—Guillaume. So call me Willy. I love you very dearly. I will marry you as soon as we land. Of course, *ma femme* and my six children will object, but all the same—"

"Oh, be quiet, will you?" Kathy said. "When do we get there?"

"Now," Willy said, and banked the Apache vertically so that one torpedo-shaped wingtip tank raced across the landscape. He was right: Paris was below. Kathy could see the Tour Eiffel, and les Invalides. Willy eased up on the vertical bank a little, holding twenty-seven degrees, and the bridges of the Seine swam backward beneath them and there were Notre-Dame and La Conciergerie; and the Louvre, and the Bastille, and the pastel iced cake of Sacré-Coeur. They went over Paris so low that Kathy could pick out the Gare du Nord and after that the Gare St. Lazare and then the Grands Boulevards, and the Etoile with the Arc de Triomphe sitting in the middle of it and the Rond-Point and the Place de la Concorde with its fountains and obelisk and the Madeleine and—

She turned back to Willy.

"We seem to be making *le grand tour*," she said.

"We are," the Belgian pilot said; and for once his voice was grim. "It is that I wished to reassure myself, Mademoiselle Kathy. When we passed over *Le Bourget*, the tower, which is manned by the *militaire* since the civilian radio operators are on strike, too, warned me there might be more trouble. There was last night. A considerable amount of it. So I wished to see if there were mobs in the streets . . ."

He grinned at her, suddenly.

"Unfortunately, there are not, so I have no excuse to fly you back to Liège where I have *'tit apartement que ma femme* does not know about and—"

"I told you I have a husband," Kathy said.

"And I—a wife. Which makes us even. Let's forget them, shall we?"

"Can't," Kathy whispered. "It so happens that I love mine, Willy."

"*Tant pis,*" Willy said, and lifted the Apache's shark-shaped nose, the twin propellers catching the light, making blinding disks suddenly, heading southward, the turbines whining as though they, too, were eager to get it over with. Toward Orly.

Then they were sliding down through layers of cotton batten and fleece and lace, and all the noises changed. Willy lowered the flaps, and Kathy heard the rumbling thud as the tricycle landing gear dropped out of its niches in the wings and the nose of the plane and locked into place. The whine of the turbines was shriller now, more urgent, and the tower was ballooning up to their left; she could see the runway, oil-streaked and gray, a few meters below them, then the tires screeched, screamed, and they were racing over the ground at unbelievable speed, until abruptly Willy reversed the pitch of the props and gunned the turbines at the same time so that the whole world went hideous with noise. The Apache shuddered, slowed, became a captive of earth again, heavy, lumbering, tired, out of its element now, chained by the forces it had for some hours overcome.

Like me in New York, Kathy thought. But I'll fly again. With him, I'll fly. That is, if I can find him. And I'll do that, too, because I've got to. I've got to! You hear me, God?

Willy taxied the trim little twin-turbine Apache up to the ramp. Cut the motors. Sat there grinning at her. But he didn't open the doors. Kathy wondered what he was waiting for. She had already paid him the quite outrageous fare he had demanded of her in Brussels, before they'd even taken off.

"Let me out of here, Willy!" she said.

"That will cost you a little more," Willy said.

"How much?" Kathy said, her voice shaking with anger.

"One little kiss," Willy said. "*C'est tout, ma belle!*"

It wasn't worth fighting over, Kathy decided. So she kissed him and got out of there. Willy got down and unlocked the baggage compartment. He handed her down her bags, one by one. Then he tried to kiss her again, but she sidestepped him nimbly. He grinned at her, a little sadly.

"*Tant pis*," he said, and climbed back into the plane.

After he had gone, racing down the runway in a blast of propwash that threatened to tear all her clothes off, Kathy stood there forlornly on the ramp and waited for a porter to come and take care of her luggage. None did. Nor did she see Fats, whom she'd phoned just before leaving Brussels. But then she scarcely expected to. It would take him longer to get out to the airport than the little Apache had taken from Belgium to Paris. So she did what she had to: She took her bags, two at a time, up to the door marked "Police." Then she stood there, trembling and panting a little.

The uniformed policeman looked at her passport a long time. Then he stamped it. After that, he craned his neck out of his booth and stared at her bags.

"*La Douane* is over there," he said.

Kathy wanted to cry. Anywhere else on earth, she raged inside her mind, a policeman, knowing there are no porters, would help me with my bags. Discourtesy, they name is France!

Then she did it all over again, hauling and dragging her bags up to the customs bench. The *douanier* marked them all with his piece of chalk without asking her to open even one of them, as sometimes, capriciously, Parisian *douaniers* do.

Hoping against hope, she looked around for a porter to take her bags to a taxi. As she expected, there weren't any. She turned back to the customs man.

"*Est-ce que il n'y a pas—?*" she began.

"*Les porteurs? Non*, Mademoiselle. They're on strike. The taxis, *aussi*. The autocars, likewise. All the world is on strike *sauf que nous et les flics, ma toute petite fille . . .*"

"But how on earth am I going to get into Paris?" Kathy wailed.

"*Si vous êtes folle,* you can walk. Or *faire le auto-stop.* It is merely fifteen kilometers—no, nearer twenty. Of the two, walking is wiser. *Les types* who still have gas for their automobiles are usually crooks who operate on the black market, and, hence are not to be trusted with a pretty little thing like you. But if you are truly *une jeune fille sage,* you will march yourself to the airport's hotel and rest there until tomorrow. You look too fatigued to attempt to walk into Paris today—"

"But I have to get to Paris *today!* I have to!" Kathy said.

"No you do not, *ma fille,*" the *douanier* said. "For that is not at all wise. I, myself, plan to stay out here tonight instead of going home. Paris, unhappily, will be, I'm afraid, more dangerous than it was ten days ago . . ."

"Why?" Kathy said.

"The Government has fobidden the return of Cohn-Bendit from Germany," the customs official said. "And, already, this morning, the students were gathering. They are even angrier than before—and better prepared. For example, this morning, they were listening at the Gare de Lyon to the discourses of the little red Danny *enregistrés en magnétaphone*—tape recorders you call them, *hein?*—in Germany, and sent back by special courier. What is that if not organization? Tonight there will be trouble, and it will be grave. *Ecoutez ce vieillard,* Mademoiselle. *Je vous previens que—*"

"No," Kathy said. "My husband is in the Latin Quarter. I must go to him."

"Then, Mademoiselle—I beg pardon, Madame—has only to walk—and to pray."

"*Merci*, M'sieu," Kathy said, and left him there.

Ten minutes later, she was standing in the waiting room, surrounded by her luggage. But her mind was working very coldly and very well.

She bent, and with quite astonishing strength, lifted the biggest bag up on one of the benches. Fishing in her purse, she came out with a bunch of keys. But once she had the bag open, all she took out of it was a pair of flat-heeled loafers. She kicked off the spike-heeled shoes she was wearing, and put on the loafers. Then she put the shoes in the big bag, closed and locked it. After that she opened her *nécessaire*. Out of it she took a stick of deodorant, a tiny flask of perfume, her toothbrush and toothpaste, some cleansing tissue, and put them into her purse, which made it bulge considerably. As she closed the *nécessaire*, she caught a sheen of pale blue in the oblique tangent of residual vision, and, looking again, she saw that it was a box of Tampax. The corners of her mouth flickered upward into a wan and wry grin.

Damned if this isn't the first time in my life that I actually wish I needed the blamed things, she thought. Then she locked the little overnight case, picked it and another bag up, and started towards the storage room where there were lockers for hire. It took her three trips to dispose of her luggage; and by then she was half dead of exhaustion; but she was operating on the basis of sheer nerve now and had been for at least three days, so she wasn't aware of how tired she was.

She started out from Orly, walking. She kept on walking until she came to a filling station. She thought she'd wait there to see if she could hitch a ride into Paris; but then she saw that the place was deserted and all the pumps bore the crudely lettered announcement, *"Pas d'essence"*—"Out of Gas."

So she moved on. Five kilometers farther along, a car drew up beside her.

"Paris?" the driver said.

"Oui, M'sieu," Kathy said.

He leaned across the seat and opened the door.

"Entrez," he said.

"Merci, M'sieu," Kathy said.

Half a kilometer later, he put his hand on her leg. Not on her knee, but on the inner thigh, as high up as he could reach.

"You will have the goodness to remove it, your hand," Kathy said.

He grinned at her and shook his head, showering ashes down his shirt front from the *Gauloise Bleue* that was glued to his lower lip.

"Comme vous êtes drôle, vous," he said. "I know why *le bon Dieu* made *les petites blondes.*

"And why did He?" Kathy said, reasonably enough.

"Pour moi," the driver said. "For me."

Then he shoved his big, beefy hand all the way up between her thighs, using considerable force to do it.

Kathy didn't hit him. Not then. First she repeated the maneuver which in a certain sense could be called the first cause of her present troubles: She leaned forward suddenly and jerked the key out of the ignition; but this time, instead of dropping it down the front of her dress, she threw it out of the window as hard and far as she could.

The driver screamed in pure anguish. Because, as Kathy had already lived in France long enough to learn,

Frenchmen tolerate their wives, lust after their mistresses, and love their cars.

"*Salope!*" he howled. "*Petite garce! Espèce de putain tartignole qui—*"

Then his rage at this desecration of the sacred object, this mechanical idol that had cost him so much work and sacrifice, that had elevated him, in his own eyes at least, to the altitude of a *grand séducteur*, overcame him. His face blue with fury, he lunged at Kathy—which was his mistake.

Kathy swung her handbag. The things she had crowded into it at the airport lent it considerable weight. And it had behind it a good many invisible forces: all her own outrage at fate's cumulative addition of dirty tricks, all her stored-up anguish, confusion, anger, pain. It caught her would-be seducer full in the face, and broke his nose.

The expression of shock, of astonishment even, that loosened his countenance then, at being confronted with a woman with guts enough to hit back—which was against all the rules he lived by—was actually ludicrous; but when he put his hand to his nose and it came away covered with his own blood, even that expression changed, became self-pity, became woe, and he blubbered like a child.

By that time, Kathy was out of the Peugeot, and running hard. She might as well have saved her strength and her breath. Her knight in shining mechanical armor had neither the intention nor the will to follow her.

Two kilometers farther along, breath gone and sobbing, she leaned up against a telephone pole and waited for Fats Winkler to reach her, from the five hundred meters away that she had been able to recognize him, puffing along on his little red bike, like the mountain to Muhammad come.

By the time they reached Paris it was night.

"Where do I take you, baby girl?" Fats said.

"Harry's place—if you don't mind, Fats," Kathy whispered. "I—I still have the key . . ."

"Lord God, baby," Fats groaned, "didn't they tell you at the airport that the students—"

"Yes, Fats. But if I go anywhere else and he came back home and—"

"There you've got something, baby," Fats said. "But now you tell me, how the ever-lovin' hell are we going to get to the Rue Monsieur le Prince without getting our heads beat in? Paving stones or *matraques*, don't make no never mind. We go through the quarter and we've had it, Kathy. Them kids are out to wreck Paris and overthrow the government on top of that—"

"Stop here," Kathy said.

"Here?" Fats said.

"Yes. That's a *tabac* over there, and it's open. I'm going to buy a streetmap of Paris. That way we can figure out the safest way—"

"Baby," Fats groaned, "there ain't any, but for Harry's sake, I'm game . . ."

"But not for mine, eh, Fats?" Kathy said sadly. "Still don't believe in me, do you?"

Solemnly Fats bent down and kissed her on the forehead.

"Don't know what happened 'twixt you 'n Harry," he said. "Don't even want to. You came back, and that's what counts. From now on, in my book, you're the greatest, girl baby. Now scoot. Go buy your map before I really give out . . ."

"Thank you, Fats," Kathy said and fled.

She planned their route very well indeed. It was roundabout, but they were never in any danger at all. They came into the city by the Avenue de Choisy, crossing the Place d'Italie, and continuing up the Avenue des Gobelins until they got to the Boulevard de Port-Royal. There they turned left and crossed the Boule Mich' at the place where it ends. But, instead of entering the Boulevard Montparnasse—sure to be as filled with *enragés* as St. Michel, itself—they angled northwestward across the Place Julian, and went up the Rue d'Assas until its intersection with Guynemer. Taking that street, they went three-quarters of the way around the Luxembourg Gardens, turning right off Guynemer into Vaugirard until finally they came to Rue Monsieur le Prince, where Harry lived.

By then, it was well after midnight of May 24, 1968, and from the fashionable Rue de Rivoli on the Right Bank, to the Bourse, from the Bastille to the Gare de Lyon, from the intersection with Raspail to the Pont Sully on St. Germain, from one end of the Boulevard St. Michel to the other, all of Gay-Lussac, St. Jacques, and a hundred places more, Paris was aflame.

Rue Monsieur le Prince begins at the Carrefour de l'Odéon and ends at the Boulevard St. Michel. Somebody had ordered the police to respect the Odéon, itself, which was still occupied by the students and had been since May 13. So all Kathy and Fats encountered on Monsieur le Prince were *enragés* clad in the helmets and bearing the shields of Roman gladiators, this ancient but remarkably effective armor having been stolen from the scenic wardrobe of the theater. But they could hear the gasoline tanks of the cars on the Rue des Saints-

Pères, St. Germain, and the Boule Mich' exploding as
the students deliberately tossed Molotov cocktails under
those hated symbols of bourgeois materialism.

"They're wrong," Fats said. "They don't know their
own people, them kids. Lord, looks like living here all
their lives they'd know you can touch a Frenchie's old
lady, but please for Chrissake leave his car alone!"

"That's what they hate," Kathy said softly. "This—
this living for *things*. Like cars. Like houses. Like re-
frigerators and TV sets and transistors. Making a slave
out of oneself for what doesn't matter at all, instead of
for what does. Like—love, Fats. Like being—happy, or
trying to. Like—people—like my Harry. If he still is, that
is. Oh, Fats, I—"

"Baby," Fats said, "you been listening to that Levi
cat too hard. But I'll buy that lovin' 'n being happy bit.
Now come on . . ."

They stood in front of the ancient and grimy apartment building.

"You want me to walk upstairs with you, girl baby?"
Fats said.

"Would you?" Kathy said. "It—it's so dark. And I *am*
scared, a little. But once I get inside, I'll be all right . . ."

"Wait a sec," Fats said. "Got to hide my lil' red *vélo*
in the hall, or one of them enraged cats will confiscate
it for the good of the cause . . ."

"All right," Kathy said.

Fats dragged the bicycle across the *trottoir*. Kathy had
a key to the downstairs door as well. Harry had given her
one out of his weary knowledge of how Parisian con-
cierges react to being wakened in the middle of the night
to let a belated lodger in. Fats bumped the bike over
the doorsill and into the hall. Then he touched the but-

ton of the *minuterie*, the invention of French frugality that puts the lights on and then cuts them off again before anyone has a chance to walk up even half a flight of stairs. When the dim, yellowish, undersized lights flickered on, he took Kathy by the arm and started up the stairs.

Which was why he saw, witnessed, even suffered through what happened next.

As usual, the lights went out, just as they reached the door of Harry's flat. Fats groped around the wall in an effort to find the *minuterie* button on that floor. But what he touched was the bell.

It shrilled, hideously. Fats swore under his breath. Found the light button. The lights flickered on again. Kathy bent towards the keyhole once more. Froze into immobility. For, by then, both she and Fats had heard the footsteps coming on.

"Harry!" Kathy breathed, but that was all she had time for, because the door opened—cautiously at first, just a little—then swung wide.

"*Va t'en, respectueuse! File!* March yourself," Ouija Zahibuine said.

Chapter
Twelve

Kathy stood there, staring at the girl. She didn't say
anything. She couldn't. She just stood there. She didn't
even breathe.

Ouija had on Harry's bathrobe. Her lips were blue-
bruised, swollen. A thin trickle of blood had crept down
from one corner of her mouth. And, as if to confirm
what needed no further confirmation, she smelled like
the morning after a busy night in *une maison close*,

which is what the French call a brothel when they're in a mood to be polite. A cheap *maison close*. Located in les Halles, say.

"Baby—" Fats groaned.

But, by then, Kathy had already whirled and was running down the stairs.

"Kathy!" Fats cried out, and started to go after her; but Ouija reached out and took his arm.

"Let her go," she said. "Perhaps they'll kill her out there. Then I'll be free of her. Then I keep him—keep Harry. *Peut-être.* Oh, Fats, *comme la vie est moche!*"

And to Fat's total confusion, Ouija bent her head and cried.

"Ouija, honey," he got out, "preaching ain't my bit. But laying a guy when he's mean mad and hurt is plumb, downright foolish. And him married at that. Not to mention what your Pa—"

"*Je ne te comprends pas,*" Ouija said. "*Pas du tout, Fats. Parle français, veux-tu?*"

"Oh, Jesus!" Fats said. "Ouija, *chèrie, j'ai dit que—*"

Then he heard Harry's footsteps, limping heavily, coming on.

Fats stood there, looking at him.

"You poor bastard," he said. "You poor, poor bastard."

"Kathy," Harry said dully, "you said, 'Kathy.' I heard you, Fats."

"Yep," Fats said. "Sure Lord did, soul brother. She *was* here. Brung her in from Orly on my little red bike. She come back—all ready, willin', and eager to make a go of it. To put up with what a poor dumb gray chick has to when she's hitched to a spade. Only she didn't figger on finding you shacked up so fast. 'N specially not with lil' Ouija here—"

"She—she came back—" Harry said. "She came back—" His voice rose suddenly, went shrill, broke, shattered like crystal. "Oh, Christ!" he said, and hurled himself down the stairs.

Ouija stood there. Shook her head very slowly.

"So—she has won again," she said harshly. "This pale little *poule*. This species of a *garce*. *Cette très petite chose, moche blèche, tartignole; mais en dépit de tout ça elle a gagné, et moi*—I have lost him. *Pourquoi*, Fats? Tell me that. Why? In Allah's name, why?"

"Don't know," Fats said. "Perhaps because she is—special, too. In her own way. She is *une fille galante*, Ouija. *Très, très galante*. Do you not comprehend this, *ma pauvre petite?* She has had to go against everything she has been taught, everything she has thought, believed, everything her ancestors have handed down to her in three centuries, *ma belle*—in order to even *see* Harry as a man. And yet—"

"She does see him. And—loves him. Which is a thing that seems to me *drôlement facile*. Fats, take me in your arms. Hold me."

"*Moi?*" Fats said.

"Yes, you. Or else I'll scream. You see—they—they—stabbed Raoul tonight. Before my eyes. I think that he is dying or already dead. And after that, they—please, Fats, hold me. Please."

"Oh Jesus!" Fats said, and took her in his arms.

Harry went straight down Monsieur le Prince in the

direction of the Boulevard St. Michel. He knew it was foolish to run, but he ran all the same. Before he had gone a block, he was sweating, cool as the night was. That helped, though. The last of the gut-rotting mixture of cognac, gin, whiskey, pernod, beer, champagne, *vin ordinaire*, and other nameless concoctions made of garbage, glue, and floor varnish, probably, he'd drunk over the last four days came out through his pores.

She'll go there, he thought. Where it's bad. Goddamned bad. Lord awful. Looking for that way out. And even if I find her in time, what can I say that she'll believe? The truth? Ha! With all that first-class circumstantial evidence against it? Hell, I wouldn't believe that one myself, and I know it's so. Just try it on for size: 'Look, Kathy baby, I've been stoned four days. Blind, stinking drunk. Because you took yourself an airy-plane and the breeze from its jets blew me clean off the world. Don't know how I got home. Don't even know where I've been. The only thing I do know is whoever the horny, hamfisted, mother-loving son of a bitch was who rough-humped little Ouija, it sure as hell wasn't me.' Tell Kathy that. Tell her Ouija got to my pad not ten minutes before she did. Hell, I was still seeing four of that poor baby-girl child, bruised all over, ripped open down there, and bleeding like a pig when Fats started punching the bell and yelling in the hall. Tell Kathy that. Prove to that sweet innocent that that's how things usually operate in this miserable, fucked-up world; that coincidence's only function is to force you to assume the position: on your hands and knees with your asshole sucking air. And that fate's not three old funky bitches with a ball of string, a ruler, and some scissors, but a heavy-hung, rough old fag out to do a reaming job on every poor shitty bastard born.

He went on running jerkily, a sort of skipping hop to favor his bad leg, until he could see the boulevard. It wasn't pretty. The garbage men had been on strike for nearly two weeks now, and Paris was one huge, reeking dump. But now the students had poured gasoline all over the mounds of stinking debris that reached in some places to the height of the second-story windows, and set them afire. Everywhere he looked, the night belched flame, with black silhouettes dancing in and out of it and howling.

He heard again the whistling whine of the ball bearings and the nuts and bolts the students were shooting from their slingshots at the CRS. The sodden crunch of paving stones. The coughing bark of the flics' grenade launchers. The crash and splatter of Molotov cocktails. The dull boom of a car's gas tank going, the air gone solid from the explosion, slamming against his eardrums on the nearer side like a fist.

He looked at the car: a Deux Chevaux, the cheapest and ugliest automobile in the world. Belongs to a worker, likely, he thought; to some poor bastard who's broke his everloving balls getting the sous together to buy that heap. Now look at it. That's how to lose a revolution, not win it, you lovely people, you . . .

But, by then, the flames had gutted the little Citroën, so he went on. Afterwards, he didn't know, couldn't even remember all the streets he'd gone through with his hands folded over his head to protect it a little from all the flying objects that threatened every second to knock his brains out.

The brains I don't even have, he thought, 'cause if I did, I sure as hell wouldn't be in the middle of this out-sized screwup. Then: Goddamn', but these cats are organized!

They were. Not many of them were bareheaded any-more. Aside from the few who bore Roman, Greek, and medieval helmets and shields stolen from l'Odéon's wardrobe, and were, as a result, constantly bathed in the white lightnings of the foreign newspapermen's flash cameras, for being, as Harry put it bitterly, so god-damned cute, most of the *enragés* had on motorcyclists' leather helmets and heavy winter coats, which took a good bit of the force out of a *matraque*'s murderous blows. And he saw another thing, too. The most effec-tive fighters weren't the students but the young workers from Paris' red belt, the grimy, miserable factory towns that surround *la ville lumière*. And even better were the young hoods, that special Gallic brand of not-so-juvenile delinquents whom the Parisians call *Blousons Noirs* from their self-adopted uniform: black, close-fitting leather jackets. They were accounting for two out of three of the policemen felled.

What the students were good at, Harry saw, was de-fensive tactics. The barricade at the intersection of the Rue des Saints-Pères, built under the direction of the engineering students, was a real chef d'oeuvre; and the chemists of the *l'Ecole Polytechnique et l'Ecole de Pharmacie*, had come up with a simple but remarkably effective countermeasure against tear gas: handkerchiefs soaked in a solution of lemon juice and bicarbonate of soda. Harry found that out, because, seeing his black face, they at once assumed he was one of the African students, and handed him one, saying:

"*Mettez ça sur la bouche et le nez, mon gars. Ça marche contre le gas lacrymose . . .*"

It did march. His eyes stung less badly now. But he couldn't give all the credit to the improvised gas masks, because the students' other tactics against the gas grenades had reduced the amount of the hateful yellowish-white fumes in the air to an absolute minimum. Squads of them, armed with fire extinguishers robbed from every nearby building, wet down every OF grenade as soon as it fell, while still others were using the lids of garbage pails to smother them before they could even begin to blow.

But the *Compagnies Républicaines de Sécurité*, the *Gardes Mobiles*, the *Police d'Intervention*, and the ordinary flics—so-called from their nasty habit of "flicking" a suspect with their capes, which, since said capes have lead sewn into their hems, often left said suspect missing an eye, or spitting out a mouthful of his own teeth —had improved a good bit themselves. Now they carried round sheet-iron shields, strangely resembling the Roman and Greek shields the students had borrowed from l'Odéon, except that they weren't ornamented. But they kept ninety per cent of the ball bearings, nuts and bolts, paving stones, ax handles, sewer gratings, and other sundry heavy objects from making contact with the policemen's heads. The *Gardes*, CRS, and ordinary flics all wore leather helmets, goggles, and gas masks, giving the whole thing the aspect of a diabolically fantastic Orson Welles *The War of the Worlds* script, except that the blood that was flowing was real.

The pharmacy students, and the medical school's still-to-be doctors and nurses were taking care of the wounded with complete impartiality, attending bleeding flics as tenderly as moaning *enragés*, thus making the whole thing rather sporting. Or adding to its Ionesco-Beckett type aburdity, Harry thought.

By that time, he was back on the Boulevard St. Michel again. He didn't even know how he'd got there. By the great-circle route, he thought grimly; via Alaska over the North Pole. But it had been more nearly via hell through purgatory.

"I'm beat," he muttered. "I'm dead beat and if I don't find her soon, I'm gonna cave in. And if I do, what? Half a week on a liquid diet, and that liquid rot-gut sure as hell isn't calculated to—"

Then he saw the student medics carrying a girl. A small blonde girl who hadn't any face. All she had was a Grand Guignol mask of thick, ropey, dripping red, out of which her great blue eyes peered in utter astonishment.

He stood there. What he wanted to do, and what he could do, were suddenly two different things—or three. He wanted to go to her. To bend over her and say word-less, impossibly tender, things. To comfort her. To put his arms around her and make everything all right—even that hideously battered face. But his legs wouldn't move. His gut churned. A solid, scalding rush of nausea hit the back of his throat; his eyes went out of focus, blurred the world, extinguished it.

"No," he said. "No. Get a grip on yourself, son. That's it. That's it. Go to her. Say—"

But what came out of his mouth was a scream, high, ululant, woman-shrill.

"Kathy!" he wailed.

Those almost disembodied eyes rolled slowly in his direction. By the light of the blazing barricades, burning garbage, flaming cars, he couldn't tell if they were green-ish-blue like Kathy's or just plain blue; but their whites were ghostly ghastly in her shattered ruin of a face.

Then he was bending over her moaning, keening, weeping.

"Kathy. Kathy. Kathy, baby. Oh, Kathy—"

From amid all that blood, a mouth appeared. Made something appalling that was supposed to be a smile. That *was* a smile, finally. Gallant and very brave and somehow gay.

"*Suis pas*—Kathy," a contralto voice mumbled, blowing bubbles in her own blood. "*Suis* Lisette—"

"Oh, thank God!" he said in English. Then, "*Merci*, Lisette. *Ca vaut bien peu, mais j'espère que vous*—"

"*C'est rien*," she murmured. "*Va t'en, mon brave. Trouvez—votre*—Kathy. *Et depuis—depuis—*"

He bent closer. Her bearers had stopped, thinking him a lover, or a friend.

"*Depuis—quoi?*" he said.

"*Dites-lui—de ma part qu'elle a—elle a vraiment de la chance!*"

He took her hand. Opened his mouth to say—what? What were the words? What could he say to this unknown, who'd handed him back his reason and perhaps his life, that would mean anything? And what right had he, anyhow, to—

It was then he heard the crash as the first of the bulldozers the police had brought up hit the barricades. He turned, staring at it. That beautiful chef d'oeuvre the engineering students had taken hours to build, lasted minutes before that mindless, remorseless, mechanical brute force. He stood there petrified, watching it until he became aware that among all the curses, shrieks, screams of the students stumbling, falling, crawling, running, racing away from the doomed barricade there was one voice calling his name.

It came again, fluting above the din: "Harry! Oh, Harry, I—"

Then he saw her. She had fallen, and hurt herself. She couldn't get up.

"Harry—" she moaned. "Come get me, I—"

The bulldozer came on. From the cab, armored with sheet iron, with only a slit left to guide the monster by, the driver couldn't see her. And he, Harry, couldn't move. Horror held him. Fear.

Then the wounded girl dropped his hand. Threw it away from her. Cried, "*Allez-y, beau Noir!*" and broke the spell.

He ran faster than he'd ever run before in his life. He forgot his bad leg. His limp disappeared. He got there, bent, clawed her into his arms, rolled away from that massive, murderous curved blade that was scooping up tree trunks, packing cases, overturned cars, sewer gratings, stone benches—and all the thousand, thousand odds and ends the *enragés* had used to build their barricade—as though they weighed nothing at all, and showering them down again like broken toys.

It missed him by centimeters. He came up right, bore her away from there, crooning,

"Kathy. Baby girl. My baby. 'S all right now. Now we've got it made! Now—"

"Ouija," she said. "Oh, Harry, how could you? I hate you! I hate—"

But he bent and stopped her mouth with his own.

One-half second later, the CRS man's *matraque* caught him diagonally across the face and sent him down. From where he lay, looking up into that beet-red face, he knew suddenly, coldly, absolutely that the liberal, conciliatory, non-violent concepts he'd had preached at him all his life were nonsense, absurdities, that Whitey is universal; and that the planet Earth is too small for the white race and the black together. That one of the two of them had to get off.

But Kathy was on her feet, facing the Republican Security man. Her face was ghost-white. She was shaking with pure fury.

"Why have you done that?" she said. *"Dites-moi, pourquoi?"*

The policeman grinned at her, slowly.

"Parce que," he said, *"je n'aime pas les nègres, moi.* And *un nègre* with a pretty little blonde like you, even less. *Même quand la blonde* is a foreigner like you, *petite.* I find that sort of thing *degoûtante.* How much did this big ape pay you, *'tite poule? D'advantage, j'en suis sûr, moi.* Tomorrow, when I shall be off duty, *je te payerai encore plus!"*

What Kathy did next was unwise, especially in a country where, among whose lower classes at least, beating up women is a national sport: She brought her right hand around in a wild swing. It exploded against the policeman's face with a sound like a pistol shot. The CRS man hung there, staring at her for a long, long moment before he cracked her across the side of the face with his *matraque.* By his own standards, he was almost polite. He didn't hit her very hard. But he underestimated his strength. The blow was more than enough to stretch Kathy out full-length on the ground.

Harry came up off the pavement then. He went under the *matraque's* swing and buried his left fist to the wrist in the policeman's belly. Caught the CRS man flush on the chin with a hard right as he doubled, chopped the policeman's neck with the edge of his hand as that big, beefy Porte de Lilas type went down, then finished the job with a kick that landed exactly on target between those muscular, uniformed thighs, and was designed to make that one particular *salaud* useless to women forevermore.

The execution done, the punishment administered, Harry bent to pick up Kathy. She was lying on the paving stones, holding her swollen cheek and crying very softly.

"Oh Christ!" he whispered and reached out his arms to gather her up.

But, by then it was too late. An army of security men were upon him. Their *matraques* made a forest, shutting out the firelight. He heard Kathy scream, "No! Don't! Please don't! *Ne le tuez pas, je vous prie!*" Then all the flame-shot dark gathered itself together and made *un feu d'artifice*, a fireworks show that exploded inside his head and blew his mind away.

And after that—*rien. Néant.* Nothing. Absolutely nothing at all.

Chapter
Thirteen

The CRS picked Harry up by the arms and legs and slung him headfirst into one of those big, black police vans whose grilled windows have earned them the name of *paniers à salade*, salad baskets. Kathy stood there and watched them do that. She stayed there unmoving for the next half-hour while the security men punched, kicked, slugged, and stomped another even dozen bleeding, battered hulks of both sexes into quiescence, which in most cases meant unconsciousness, and then threw them into *le saladier* on top of Harry.

But when the policemen began to climb into the paddy wagon, she realized they were going to drive away and tried to climb in with them. They wouldn't let her. "March yourself, little American whore," they said. It was, Kathy afterwards realized, the third word of that *"petite poule Americaine"* that saved her from a beating and from being arrested. The CRS wanted no complications from foreign consulates that night. They had enough on their hands as it was. So they slammed the doors of the salad basket shut, drove off, and left her there.

Kathy started walking then. She went through streets she had never even heard of before, not to mention having seen; but, as the lost always do, she traveled in a circular route, so that, just before morning, she found herself on the Boulevard St. Germain again. And because she recognized it, because it was old, familiar, loved, she stayed on it, moving away from the sounds of the fighting. She was so tired that she had gone beyond fatigue and was operating upon nothing more than her raw and screaming nerves. They, or pure will, or sheer guts, or all three, held her up while she lifted one foot, then the other, and put them down again three thousand, five thousand, ten thousand times until she came to the Pont Sully on the far end of the boulevard.

She went across the bridge and turned left onto the Right Bank *quai*. When she got to the Tuileries, she crossed the Gardens and came out on the Rue Rivoli. She went up the street under the arcades until she got to the Place de la Concorde and crossed the Place and went on up the Avenue Gabriel until she came to the American Embassy.

By then it was midmorning, so she was able to enter it. She went into the consular section and said to the receptionist,

"The Consul, please."

And something—her tone of voice, the lines, lineaments, and posture of horror into which her slight form was frozen, her utter, unvoiced and voiceless despair, came through to the clerk, so that she became the first human being in recorded history to get to see an American Consul anywhere in Europe without having to wait three-quarters of an hour. In fact, she didn't have to wait at all, but was shown into the Consul's office at once.

The Consul sat there and fiddled with his glasses while she told her story.

"We'll see what we can do," he said. "What is your address, Mrs.—"

"Forbes," Kathy said. "Mrs. Harrison Forbes. I haven't any. I just got here this morning, and I haven't had time to—"

"I see," the Consul said wearily. "Have you any money, Mrs. Forbes?"

"Yes," Kathy said. She had over five thousand dollars in her bag, because before she had left New York the bank her father did business with there had cashed a personal check for her on the strength of the Nichols name—backed up by her passport, of course. The miracle was that she hadn't lost her bag last night. It was a screamingly smart pouchlike affair with drawstrings that looped over her wrist, which was why, maybe, that she had been able to keep it without even remembering that she had it, while dodging bulldozers and fighting policemen and wandering through a curiously surrealistic imitation of hell.

"Would you like us to find you lodgings?" the Consul said.

"Yes," Kathy said. "But not at the Georges Cinq or the Plaza Athenée, please. I'm too well known at those places, and, you see, it so happens I haven't any clothes. I had to leave my bags out at the airport."

The Consul stared at her. Bruised, torn, dirty, she didn't look like the kind of person who habitually stayed at the two best hotels in Paris. But then it came to him that she probably was. Her voice, her gestures, her bearing, added up to money. Old money, in the family long enough to have started her mother and maybe even her grandmother before her off right, so that there was in her, in spite of everything, a certain ease, say, a kind of self-assurance that couldn't be counterfeit, and to the Consul's practiced eye revealed that she was one of the class of people you gave special treatment to—in defense of your job, and in hope of future promotions at the very least.

"Forbes?" he said. "The Philadelphia Forbes—or the Maryland ones?"

Kathy looked at him. Then she glanced down at the nameplate on his desk. John Dalton, First Consul, it read.

"Neither, Mr. Dalton," she said. "My husband's family is from Georgia. And since you're going to try to find him for me, I guess I'd better tell you all of it. They're Negroes. Blacks. You pick whichever word's more correct these days . . ."

The Consul opened his mouth. Closed it again. With

all his training, his recovery was nonetheless slow. Fits, he thought bitterly. It's always the best who do it now. Like the chief's daughter, for instance. What's new is that their families give in. Fashionable liberalism—or something. Oh, hell, I . . .

He let his breath out, slowly.

"Mrs. Forbes," he said, "would you mind telling me your maiden name?"

Kathy stiffened.

"I'm over twenty-one," she said.

"I didn't mean that," Dalton said. "Frankly—I'm curious. It's *still* unusual, you know. And you *do* have a drawl. Very slight, but—"

"The name's Nichols. The Cancer Merchants," Kathy said.

"The cancer merch—" John Dalton began—then he got it. "*Those* Nichols! The tobacco people! Why I'm sure I must have seen your picture in the papers fifty or a hundred times—"

"On the society page. Where they put the ornamental and the useless," Kathy whispered. "Mr. Dalton, I'm very tired. Would you be so kind as to do something about finding me a room?"

"Of course," the Consul said, and touched the bell. Almost at once, his secretary came into the office.

"See if you can find lodgings for Mrs. Forbes, here," he said. "A small, quiet place. I'd suggest you try somewhere in the sixteenth *arrondissement*. Is that all right with you, Mrs. Forbes?"

"Yes," Kathy said. It was. The sixteenth includes the Grands Boulevards, Kleber, MacMahon, Grande Armée, as well as the Rond-Point and the Etoile.

"I'll send you in one of our cars to whatever hotel we

find," John Dalton said. "But, while we're waiting, would you mind telling me a little about your husband? Wait—it's not entirely curiosity, though I'm honest enough to admit I am curious. If I'm to find him for you, I need some information about him, Mrs. Forbes. A physical description would help, and—"

"Have you ever been to Le Blue Note?" Kathy said.

"Yes. Yes, of course. Oh, I say! *That* Harrison Forbes. The clarinetist. A very fine musician. But I thought he was married to—"

"A Vietnamese girl. He was. She died. So now you know what my husband looks like."

"Yes," the Consul said. "A striking man. Very handsome indeed. Which probably explains matters, doesn't it?"

"No," Kathy said wearily. "It doesn't. What explains my marrying him is that he is kind and good and very patient with fools. I didn't even realize he was handsome until after I'd decided to marry him. For the wrong reasons—which, if he lives, I'm going to make up to him—"

"The wrong reasons?" the Consul said.

"Yes. And all the—burdens I've already piled on his shoulders. My color, or rather my lack of it. My heritage of—bigotry. Paternalistic, patronizing, benevolent—but bigotry just the same. And—my past. It'll take a lot of love to make up for all that . . ."

"I see," John Dalton said. But it was evident to Kathy that he didn't see at all. Then the secretary came through the door with a little slip of paper in her hand. With the name of the hotel written on it, of course.

From the window of the room the Consul's secretary had got her in the Hotel Splendide on the Avenue Carnot, Kathy could see the Arc de Triomphe. There were absolutely no cars at all snarling around the Etoile beneath it, which meant things were very bad indeed.

But Kathy wasn't thinking about that. She sat there, wrapped in a big towel, because she'd washed all her clothes, after having a hot bath, and hung them over the shower curtain rod to dry. She was much too exhausted to have done that, but she didn't know or realize how tired she was by then, so she did it anyhow. And that same excess of fatigue she was beyond even feeling kept her from doing what she should have, which was to have gone to bed.

Instead, she sat by the window and looked at the massive gray bulk of the Arc de Triomphe and rehearsed the speech she was going to make to Harry if he were still alive and she could find him.

"I've come back," she said. "To stay with you. To make a go of it. To be your wife. And—if you want me—you'll have to take me as I am, and hope I can learn to be what you want. No. What you need and deserve and should have. Only I'm me. Which adds up to—to twenty-two years of frivolity and uselessness and sleeping around . . ."

She drew in a breath. Let it out again. Whispered,

"My little Creep. Whom I love already, because I'm a female woman and that's the way I'm made. So you'll have to take her—him, too. That's awful. That's rotten, but what can I do? I'm sorry, Harry. But you said you could—love my baby 'cause it's mine. That you could forget how it got started. You can't, of course. Nobody could. If you came to me with Fleur's baby—or Ouija's—in your arms, I'd hate its poor innocent little guts. But you're better than I am. Finer. You've had to be, to stand the world we made for you. So you'll have to take both of us—or neither.

" 'Cause I can't give my baby up. And I can't give you up either. The only one I can give up—is me. And that means giving up both of you. No—all three of us. But that's the only alternative you've left me, now . . ."

She smiled then, put up her fingertips, and touched her mouth.

"You smashed all the other ways, out at Sens les Bains, Mister Lover Man," she whispered. "The night you killed Miss Anne. Defined—tenderness. Took all the ugliness out of what people do . . . So be alive, Harry. Don't let them have killed you. Be alive and in the world with me—so I can live, too. So we can make more babies who will be night-beautiful like you and sun-struck crazy happy wild the way I'm going to be if only— if only—"

Then she bent her head and cried. A long time and terribly. After that, she got up and went to bed.

When the telephone awakened her, she had slept a full twenty-four hours, so it was daylight again. She came awake and aware at the same time and grabbed the phone and tried to say "Hello." Only she couldn't. Fear had her by the throat so hard she was unable to make a sound.

"Mrs. Forbes?" John Dalton's voice said.

"Yes . . ." Kathy croaked.

"We've found him. He's not in prison. He's in the American Hospital at Neuilly. It seems that his employer, Monsieur Zahibuine, interceded with the authorities on his behalf and—"

Kathy sat there holding the phone and trembling. She trembled all over and her skin was blue with cold.

"Mrs. Forbes!" the Consul said sharply. "Are you there?"

"Yes!" Kathy sobbed. The tears ran down her face and danced on the corners of her mouth. They tasted as salt and bitter as old hell.

"I'll send you a car," John Dalton said. "There's still no public transportation, you know . . ."

"Would you?" Kathy whispered. "That's *very* kind of you, Mr. Dalton—"

"Don't mention it," the Consul said. "In half an hour, then?"

"No!" Kathy said. "In ten minutes, please! Five! Three! Oh, God, I—"

"Half an hour's the best I can do, my dear," the Consul said.

At the hospital, the nurse at the reception desk took Harry's card out of the filing cabinet and said:

"*Mais oui, il est chez nous. Chambre trois cents trois . . .*"

Then she stopped.

"*Mais,* Mademoiselle," she said, "*il doit y avoir une erreur quelquepart, parce que cet jeune homme est—*"

"Black. I know. I'm his wife," Kathy said.

The way the *infirmière* said "*Sa femme?*"—slanting the words upward upon a rising note of interrogation—should have warned Kathy. But it didn't. She came flying into that room where Harry lay, his black face grayish under the white turban of bandages that covered his head, without even knocking, her arms outstretched, her mouth already shaping his name.

Then she stopped. Leaned up against the doorframe. Hung there, helplessly.

Because Harry wasn't alone. Ouija Zahibuine sat in a chair beside his bed.

There was a long, long silence that stretched out to the rim edges of forever. Kathy stood there in the doorway and shook. Then she heard Harry's voice saying wearily,

"*Dis donc*, Ouija—*commence! Tu m'as promis et—*"

And Ouija, very sadly,

"*Oui, 'Arree, je te l'ai promis. D'accord.*" Then, "Kathy, *écoute-moi, s'il te plaît—*"

"No!" Kathy screamed. "I won't listen! I'm leaving—right now!"

She turned then to go; but, somehow, her legs, her feet, would not obey her sick and shuddering mind's command.

Then she felt Ouija's hand on her shoulder, and whirled, shrieking: "Don't touch me! Don't you dare!"

Then she saw the tears on Ouija's dark face, saw how terribly she cried.

She stood there, staring at Ouija. Then—maybe because she really wasn't very bright, which meant she was soft-hearted and sentimental and gentle and good (this last having absolutely nothing to do with sexual morality, for as Harry once put it, "The really poison-mean bitches always castrate a man by freezing his balls off.")— she reached out suddenly and took Ahmad's daughter in her arms.

Harry lay there, staring at the remarkable spectacle of the two of them holding each other and crying. Then he said, very quietly,

"Reckon you'll listen to me now, Kathy."

"Don't tell me!" Kathy said. "I—I'll give you up! You —you two were meant for each other anyhow—and—and even my baby's no reason to—"

"Shit," Harry said. "Tell her, Ouija."

"No!" Kathy said. "I couldn't bear it, Harry! I couldn't! I don't want to sit through an old-home confession week and—"

"Confession?" Ouija said. She got that word. It is much the same in both languages. "But what is there to confess, *ma drôle petite* Kathy? I did not make love with *ton* 'Arree. I did not because I could not. It was that night an impossibility physical. One does not couch oneself with a man—not even the man one loves—when one has been—*violée*—by four filthy brutes—ugh! how they smelled!—and so torn open *là-bas* that Doctor Moreau had to take six stiches. *Ça sera difficle* for you to believe, but I was—*vièrge* . . . I have never wanted another man —*seulement* 'Arree . . ."

"Ha!" Harry said. "How do you account for young Levi, then?"

"I was hurt. And you—were gone," Ouija said. "With —your Kathy. So—*à quoi bon la préservation de ma virginité?* I went with Raoul to his place—Ah! *Ça, non! Ça, ce n'est pas juste*—I started out with Raoul to go to his place. But we did not reach it. For *les quatre salauds de* El Fatah—*les mêmes sales types* who had threatened to *violer* me and then cut my throat—stabbed Raoul in the back. I thought he was dead, but Doctor Moreau says with any luck he will recover—so now I shall have to marry him—"

"No," Kathy said, "that no, Ouija! You don't love him, so—"

"And that has importance? I like him very much. He is a brave type, Raoul. And I—owe him some happiness, *non?* After having almost cost him his life? Anyhow, they took me to a place they had on St. Germain—above a bookstore. And there—they—did things to me. Very filthy and painful things—most of which were abnormal. I suppose we'd be there yet—*les salauds et moi*—playing turn and turn about—now this one, now that, slobbering and pawing over me—if someone had not thrown a Molotov cocktail under a little car—a *deux chevaux* Citroën that was parked in front of the *librairie*—"

"My God!" Harry said. "I saw that! And to think—no, I didn't. I couldn't have. 'Cause the one I saw was after—"

"*En tout cas, à quoi bon?*" Ouija shrugged. "They would only have knifed you, too. And besides, they had already—amused themselves with me by then. What passed was that the tank of *la petite voiture* exploded and set *la librairie* afire. The flames came climbing up the walls—so *mes quatre* heroes ran like Egyptians at the sight of an Israeli—and left me there . . ."

"You poor, poor child," Kathy said.

"*Oui, ça d'accord.* I am *une pauvre enfant, n'est-ce-pas?* A poor miserable—*petite vache,* who now knows the nature of all *vacheries* . . . The rest is *très amusant,* Kathy —*très, très drôle.* I was *toute nue*—stark-naked—and I had no clothes to put on because *les salauds* had ripped mine to pieces. In fact, they cut them off me with their knives. So I wrapped myself in the window curtains, which were very thin and transparent, and went downstairs into the street like that. And you know what passed? Nothing. *Rien du tout.* No one even looked at me. No one at all. They were all too busy fighting *cette marée de flicage*—that sea of policemen—to even look at *une fille nue.* No, worse than naked because the curtains made of me an obscenity by hiding and not hiding at the same time—*est-ce que tu comprends ça,* Kathy?"

"*Oui*—" Kathy said.

"So I went to 'Arree's. Oh, I knew where it was. Do you know why, Kathy?"

"Because you'd been there so many times before," Kathy said bitterly.

"*Oui.* To stand below in the street and look up at his window—and wish I had the courage to mount those stairs. Yet knowing he would have kicked me down them again because he has—never loved me—is perhaps incapable of loving the women of his own race—"

"*Merde,*" Harry said. "Spare me the *Cambronnement,* Ouija, *bébé.* I don't know what I'd have done if you'd paid me a visit. Maybe I'd have remembered that you're the daughter of *un grand type* who, more than *mon patron,* is my friend. And maybe not. What man knows that? The only thing that got between us, *ma très belle*— was that I was in no mood to love anyone after Fleur died . . ."

"Not even *ta* Kathy?" Ouija said.

"Especially not *ma* Kathy—whom, as a matter of fact, I didn't even like. She can tell you that. I used to torment her terribly . . ."

"You still do," Kathy whispered. "You're doing it now —talking about me as though I weren't even here . . ."

"You have nothing to preoccupy yourself about, Kathy," Ouija said. "*Rien du tout.* For when I came into his flat, like that—the door wasn't even locked—he was sitting there with his clarinet, playing "*Petite Fille*

Perdue" and crying. And he was drunk. *Ivre. Sous.*
I was making him coffee when you came. And of this
all *si misérable,* not-so *drôle histoire,* there is only one
thing—apart from *mon pauvre* Raoul's getting half-
killed, *bien entendu*—that I regret, truly—"

"And that is?" Kathy said.

"That what you so clearly thought wasn't true," Ouija
said. *"Et maintenant, je m'en vais.* Papa is removing us
to Switzerland. It is—safer, there, he thinks. And I still
have to visit Raoul *ce matin. Donc, je t'ai tout dit. La
vérité. Pourquoi la vérité est-elle si moche,* 'Arree? Why
is truth so ugly?"

"Don't know," Harry said. Then, *"Au 'voir, brave
enfant—"*

Ouija bent swiftly and kissed him; then she straightened up.

"Non, 'Arree—not *au 'voir. C'est adieu,"* she whispered. Then, in a staccato of clicking heels, she was gone.
Hauling, Harry thought, all that slightly used—gallantry
—the hell out of here. Leaving another empty space in
my big gut, or where my ass grabs, or—to quote all the
nice, sweet, clean-talking people—in my heart . . .

He lay there, looking up at Kathy.

"Well, baby girl—" he said. "Where do we go from
here?"

"Don't know," Kathy said. Then, "Harry—"

"Yes, baby girl?"

"If—if *our* first one's a girl, can I name her—Ouija?
I'd like to. 'Cause I think she's—perfectly grand."

Harry lay there, staring up at her, and wondering why
the joy wouldn't come, why all he felt was pain. His
mind peered away from her down a steep, oblique,
descending tangent. The future you could call it, he

thought; the autumnal years. I've got her now. Got my Kathy, and what does it mean? The kid, for one thing. Her little bundle. More dues. But you never get through paying, do you? For the privilege of hurting. For the pain of drawing breath. Well, I've bought the package, so I'll have to stand it. Poor little bastard. Damned if *I'll* make him pay for his origins, because if there's anything that sporting a black hide teaches you, it is that dues laid on for the accidents of existence are always too goddamned high. So the kid is one of the things it means. Rough. But bearable. Another? Perpetual exile, because I sure Lord can't dump on her what our living in the States together would be like. The definition—no, the elaboration of hell. It'll be rough enough here in France, because what all the starry-eyed and blessedly noble cats who're trying to solve the race problem leave out is that sparrows peck a bluejay to death if they can catch him, and even a mutation like a black panther is driven out of the leopard tribe. Prejudice is as old as the world, as natural, as enduring; it's justice, brotherhood, love, that are the freakouts of the race of man—

He looked at her, not seeing her really, thinking bleakly:

Do I love her, really? Love—not as opposed to, but over and beyond and even *after*, a good screw? Or do I just feel sorry for her because she really is a little lost? As who isn't? Who the everloving, mother-gripping hell ever found me? Oh, Jesus, I . . .

Then he heard the ragged intake of her breath, and her face came clear. She was crying, almost soundlessly. Her eyes weren't there. All he could see was the shift and flicker and downrush of her tears.

"You—you don't want me!" she whispered. "You

really don't! You're sorry I came back! So I'll never have —my little Ouija—'cause you—"

He took her in his arms then, thinking, pity is the better part of love anyhow and—

Then it came back. At the touch of her, as though her soft, trembling warmth were the essential ingredient to revive it: the joy he could neither contemplate nor really bear because it was one of those feelings that crossed the line of demarcation between pain and pleasure and what it felt like was a blade. He hung there quivering, blind, and on the edge of shock from the murderous sweetness of it.

"Harry," she was saying, "please don't send me away. Please don't. Please. I couldn't bear it. I really couldn't bear it. Not now. Not anymore. Even though it means you'll have to take my little Creep, too, I've *got* to stay. Please. You hear me, Harry? I said—"

Then she didn't say anything else. She looked at him and saw she didn't need to. They didn't even kiss. They just sat there on the bed holding each other and being quiet.

Because, quite suddenly, they both knew it was going to work. To go on. In spite of everything. That even after it did go flat, became routine, descended to the level of boredom all marriages get to, sooner or later, even if it went bad in any of the ten thousand different ways most legally sanctioned matings do, they'd hold on, endure, cling to each other.

Pride would see to that. The knowledge that admission of failure to a world that confidently expected and freely predicted that failure, didn't even exist as an alternative for them, that there weren't any alternatives that wouldn't be infinitely more lacerating, hurtful, destructive than anything they could do to each other, would safeguard them. Therefore, they would be very careful of each other, until that care became a condition of living, and even a substitute for at least, if not actually a means of preserving, the tenderness they now felt.

So they could be quiet. Tomorrow—and tomorrow—and tomorrow—there would be time for such a word.

The End

Madrid, Spain   May 8, 1969

ABOUT THE AUTHOR

Frank Yerby, who was born in Augusta, Georgia, in 1916, now lives in Spain. He was educated at Haines Institute, Paine College, Fisk University, and the University of Chicago. In 1947, the publication of his first book, THE FOXES OF HARROW, brought him instant recognition and he has since published twenty-one other best-selling novels, several of which have been made into films. SPEAK NOW is his twenty-third book.